Bang:
B-Squad Book Two

AVERY FLYNN

ISBN Print: 978-0-9964763-5-5

DEDICATION

"Drama is very important in life: You have to come on with a bang."
- Julia Child

bang1
baNG/
verb
1. strike or put down (something) forcefully and noisily, typically in anger or
in order to attract attention.

www.averyflynn.com/books

ACKNOWLEDGMENTS

There are so many people who help take a book from idea to reality. Trust me, no author does it alone…we're too distracted looking at hot dude pictures on the internet—for research purposes, of course. :) A huge thanks going out to Kimberly Kincaid. She edited this book and by doing so didn't just save my bacon, she saved my whole pig. I owe you girl. To Robin Covington, thank you for always having the answers to my random questions. As always, hugs and kisses going out to the entire Flynn family who love me even when I'm on deadline. Trust me, there is no greater love than that. And for the Flynnbots—even the ones who hated Tamara after Brazen—y'all make my life more fun.

xoxo,
Avery

CHAPTER ONE

Tamara

If someone had told Tamara Post a month ago that she'd be in one of Fort Worth's most exclusive members-only clubs sipping champagne at her ex-husband's Taz's engagement party, she would have laughed in that person's face. If they'd have said she'd be working as the office manager at B-Squad Security and Investigations—which her ex-husband's fiancée, Bianca Sutherland, owned—and loving it, she would have punched them square in the nose. Ex-beauty queens and former soon-to-be trophy wives didn't roll that way.

It was funny how life turned out.

Settling in on the velvet-covered settee in the Corsair Club's private party room, she contemplated getting another glass of wine from the open bar.

"Looking for one of these?" The man belonging to the deep bass voice held out a glass of her favorite chardonnay.

Whereas everyone else in the room was dressed in designer suits and glittering cocktail dresses, the tall, dark and handsome man in front of her was in pressed Wranglers, cowboy boots and a crisp white dress shirt. If he'd had a tie or a sports coat on at one time, he'd ditched them a while ago, judging by how his shirtsleeves were rolled halfway up his corded forearms. Not that she noticed that, or had scoped out the way his broad shoulders filled the shirt to perfection, or was tempted to ask him to turn around so she could confirm that his ass looked as good in those jeans as she imagined.

Men were no longer on her to-do list. But wine? Yeah, that she could do.

"Thank you." She took the glass and drank a sip.

The man sat down beside her, his brawny frame taking up most of the bench she wasn't already parked on. One of his jeans-clad legs brushed against her bare knee and, for the first time in months, a wave of warm desire had her clenching her thighs together.

Unable to figure out how to inch away to allow for space between them without being obvious about it, she crossed her legs. The move made her emerald-green skirt slide up her thigh a bit more than she was comfortable with under the circumstances. Still, giving him a glimpse of skin was less...unsettling...than actually touching him.

"I don't think we've been properly introduced." He held out his hand. "I'm Isaac Camacho."

She knew that name, and now she'd have a face to go with it every time she entered in expense reports. "You work with B-Squad."

He nodded. "On a come-and-go basis as a freelancer."

"Why's that?" From the number of B-Squad clients she'd had to turn away in the past month, Tamara knew the team could use another member.

"I've been told I don't play well with others."

His grin did something funny to her stomach.

"Now that really is too bad. It's important to play nice—mostly." It came out before she could stop it. Damn it. She didn't flirt. Not anymore. Men had been her drug of choice for too long and she'd sworn off of them.

He leaned in close. "Look, I don't want to make a scene but we need to get out of here. Now."

Her heart fluttered. She mentally rolled her eyes at herself. What could she say? Old habits died hard—even when they were oh-so-bad for her. "Why's that?"

His full lips flattened into a grim line. "There's a bounty hunter making his way through the front of the restaurant now. He's got papers on you."

Her heart stopped before kicking back on and revving into overdrive.

She had to get out of here and warn Essie.

But first she had to get rid of the guy who could be on the cover of Texas Hotties Monthly.

"That's about the worst pickup line I've ever heard in my life." She meant it to come out as dismissive, but her voice shook too much to be convincing.

"Unless you want to head back to Idaho and have to reveal to a judge exactly where Essie is so her shitbag of a cult leader father can grab her and sell her off to the highest bidder, then I suggest you get your pretty little ass up and follow me."

Her heart caught in her throat. How did he know?

She glanced around. Everyone was smiling and laughing just as they should be at an engagement party. After all the trouble she'd caused when she'd arrived and tried to extort a million dollars out of Taz, the last thing she wanted was to make any more trouble for him or the rest of the B-Squad—and that would be exactly what would happen if they got busted for knowingly harboring a fugitive. She couldn't do that to Taz, Bianca and the rest of the team.

"Why are you helping me?" She searched Isaac's face for an answer, but there were ancient languages she could decipher easier.

"I owe the team one, and I don't want a bounty hunter messing up Taz and Bianca's engagement party, because that's exactly what will happen. You know there's no way these people will let you get clapped in handcuffs and taken out of here without a fight." He shot her a flirtatious grin and stood up. "Anyway, I'm a sucker for sexy blondes who behave badly."

Glancing back at the tinted window wall separating the Corsair Club's front restaurant from the back party rooms, she could see a man in a baseball cap and jeans marching his way straight toward them.

She stood up. "Okay. How do we get out of here?"

"Just follow me, darling." He tucked her arm into the crook of his elbow. "I'll always lead you true."

Now that she highly doubted.

Isaac

Isaac Camacho shouldn't be noticing how good Tamara smelled.

One, it was weird. He was, after all, hustling through the club's hectic kitchen with one super-sexy, kinda bitchy blonde—his favorite kind—for parts unknown. He should be noticing her ass under that swishy green skirt, not something lame like the fact that she smelled like peach tea spiked with bourbon.

Two, they were dodging steaming pots and hot plates because ugly-as-roadkill bounty hunter Archie Wolczyk was hot on their heels. Even if his former life as a Recon Marine hadn't taught him the importance of survival, his stint in the county jail should have been more than enough to get an important lesson through even his thick skull: Being locked up in the pokey wasn't his style.

So instead of getting distracted by her perfume, he needed to get them both out of here before he ended up separated from the love of his life—women, all of them—for whatever stretch of jail time the judge decided aiding and abetting a fugitive deserved.

"Left." He pressed his palm against the small of her back, noting that his hand spanned almost the entirety of her waist, and guided her past the walk-in fridge and toward the employee break room.

She followed directions but shot him a quick glare over her shoulder.

Prickly little ice queen, wasn't she?

As they hurried through the break room, he ignored the surprised faces of the staff members swapping out street shoes for clogs, but gave a quick wink to the sous chef who'd given him the after-hours all-access kitchen tour a few weeks ago. Stephanie? Stacy? Selena? Sarah. That was it. Then almost as fast as he and Tamara had rushed into the break room, they were out the reinforced steel door and into the fenced-in part of the parking lot. It stank of cooking grease and rotting food from the nearby pair of Dumpsters that had been broiling in the Texas heat for the past few days. He peeked over the privacy fence, scanning the lot for the bounty hunter's backup. He spotted a couple getting out of a sedan, a valet sneaking a smoke, and a stray cat with one ear slinking between the cars.

Nothing of consequence stood between them and his truck, which was combat parked just outside the gate, ready as always for a quick getaway. He unlocked the doors with his key fob and opened the passenger door, then held out his hand to help Tamara up onto the running board. She was tall, but his oversized tires—perfect for off-roading—were no joke.

"No way." She took a step back, as if she could still escape.

It was cute.

"We don't have time for me to sweet-talk you, darlin', so let me put it this way. You either get that fine ass of yours in the truck or I'll expend the itty bitty amount of energy it would take for me to pick you up and flop you down in there."

The start of a snarl curled up one side of her mouth and she took another step back. "Look, I appreciate you giving me the heads up about the bounty hunter, but I don't know you and there's no way in hell I'm getting in your truck."

So, plan B it was.

"Okay." He held up his hands in surrender. "You've got an excellent point there."

The tension yanking her shoulders closer to her ears than they should be ebbed and her shoulders inched down a bit. That's when he scooped her up in his arms, pivoted, and dumped her into the passenger seat all before she'd even gotten a chance to let out a yelp.

"Why you—"

"Heavy-handed asshole?" He grabbed the seatbelt and dragged it down across her chest. "Giant prick?" He clicked it into place, resisting the urge to let his fingers linger on the sliver of silky skin between the top of her skirt and the bottom of her shirt that had become exposed when she'd twisted in his arms. "Handsome devil?" He flashed his patent-pending, panty-melting grin. "Big, strapping stud who can protect you?"

She didn't even flutter her long lashes. "Jerk."

"It's more succinct, I'll give you that." He shut the door and circled the front of the truck, walking a little more bowlegged than normal.

This was wrong. He should not have a hard-on while being a Good

Samaritan. Even for him, that was pretty low. She was Taz's ex-wife. She tried to extort a million dollars from him and nearly blew his relationship with Bianca straight to Timbuktu. She had Wolczyk on her ass and a teenager who she'd technically kidnapped hidden away somewhere. And on top of all that, she wasn't the least bit friendly or accommodating.

Fuck. His dick was just getting harder.

He opened the driver's side door and got behind the wheel. Tamara faced straight ahead and had her arms crossed under her impressive rack. While he was questioning his ethics, his cock was questioning his sanity because normally he would be all over her. As it was, he grit his teeth, turned the key in the ignition, and pulled into traffic.

A few months ago when Taz asked him to do some background on his ex-wife who was pretending to be his current wife, Isaac had figured it was an easy job. He'd been right and wrong. He'd turned up the arrest warrants, the information about her dead sister's ex-husband, Jarrod Fane, and the well-armed militia-like cult he ran and Tamara's allegation that the bastard had been willing to sell his only child off to one of his followers to consolidate his power base. What he hadn't discovered was where she lived, where her money was, or where she'd hidden her niece, Essie, after she'd grabbed the sixteen year old and hightailed it out of Idaho. That burned. He was a good investigator. Damn good. And she'd given him the slip. Shit. She still was and she was sitting right next to him.

He wasn't giving up though.

"How's the security at your house?" he asked, slowing down for a yellow light.

"Fort Knox."

Just that. Nothing else. He'd eaten Popsicles that had been warmer.

"That good?" Not likely. She had access to all of the B-Squad tech but that didn't mean she knew how to use it. According to Google, her talent in the eight gazillion beauty competitions she'd won had been baton twirling not setting up security systems.

"You know who's after me?" she asked, not even a nervous wobble in her voice.

"Yes, ma'am." He nodded. "Jarrod Fane. Age thirty-six. Second-generation leader of the Crest Society, with a two-hundred strong compound of armed followers and fellow nut jobs outside of Redfin, Idaho."

Oh, the arrest warrants on her came from the county judge presiding over the nasty custody case involving Essie, but there were only a few people in that area not under Fane's thumb. He was frat boy pretty, smooth and as dictatorial as any tyrant in a third world country.

If Isaac's recitation shook her, she didn't show it.

Her breathing remained as steady as her hands, folded in her lap. "Then you know I wouldn't leave a damn thing to chance."

"How did Wolczyk find you at the party?"

"Who?"

"The bounty hunter. His name's Archie Wolczyk."

"How do you know him?"

"Fort Worth isn't that big of a city. If the great state of Texas gives someone a security or investigative license and you're in the general area, I know who you are." The light turned and he merged into traffic. "So how did Wolczyk find you?"

Her cheeks turned pink. "I don't know."

So she could get ruffled—especially when it turned out she didn't know something. He tucked that bit of information away for later when he could think about what else got her all excited and bothered.

"Could he be at your house?" It's exactly where he'd be after flushing out his quarry into the open. He'd set up watch and wait for the target to scurry back to home base before taking off for the great wide open.

"No." She shook her head—firm, decisive, back in control. "I'm working at B-Squad under my name, but neither my house or my car has any link to me. Lash worked up the security system. He's the only one who knows where I live."

He breathed easier. He and Loud Mouth Lash, the B-Squad's resident security expert and sniper extraordinaire, had served together in the Marines. The man knew his shit. The house just might be Fort Knox worthy. However, there was always a way to find someone, a paper trail that would lead to the front door.

"Your name's not on the water bill? The cable? With your cell phone?"

"Nope."

So, somehow Wolczyk had gotten the jump on her connection to B-Squad. It wouldn't have been a main player, but the Devil's Dip Gym on the main floor was still active. One of those guys could have slipped. A trainer? Janitor? Guy who'd whacked off to her one too many times in the gym's cold showers? Maybe he'd followed her home one night. Maybe she'd let something slip about a neighbor.

Isaac didn't know, but he'd find out and then that little loose-lipped motherfucker would be out on his ass.

"I'll check the house out later."

Her blue eyes went wide. "*You'll* check it out?"

"As long as I'm watching out for you, you're not putting a dainty little toe inside the threshold before I give it my sign of approval."

She looked about ready to blow, but only for a second or two. Then that icy curtain came back down and she looked out her window at traffic as they inched down one of Fort Worth's always-clogged main thoroughfares, ignoring him with so much determination he considered being worried.

After a few minutes she turned in her seat to face him, the flash of what must have been her beauty queen smile nearly blinding him to oncoming traffic.

"Do we have a destination or am I too much of a weak little female to have the privilege of knowing that?" She served up that ice in a honeyed voice that was sweeter than his grandma's tea in August.

Nope. He wasn't falling into that trap. His mama had not raised a moron.

"Darlin', you are all female but not in the least little bit weak."

If she was placated by his compliment, it didn't show. "So what's the answer?"

The Majesty Movie Theater loomed up ahead on the left. The marquee advertised a show starting in ten minutes. It wasn't perfect, but it would do.

He flipped on his turn signal. "Right here."

"We're going to the movies?"

"It's the last place Wolczyk will look." The parking lot was empty, with a nice pair of open spots right by the door. He steered his truck around back anyway and reversed into a spot not visible from the road. "It's dark, no one interacts with anyone else, and they serve food."

Downtime—even watchful downtime—always meant refueling, whether food or sleep. Another lesson Uncle Sam had imparted along with sixty ways to kill a man and the importance of shower shoes.

"And after the movie?" she asked, a touch of weariness forming lines around her eyes

"We'll figure out what step to take next." He got out and hustled around to her door so he could open it for her. He made it right it in time to see her hop down without his assistance.

The look she shot him was pure sass and triumph with more than a smidgen of fuck you mixed in for good measure. His cock twitched—another good reason for sitting in the dark for a while watching some shit blow up on the screen while his dick returned to its normal not-around-Tamara state.

CHAPTER TWO

Isaac

Two hours and fourteen minutes later, Isaac wasn't sure he could walk without embarrassing himself.

Like an asshole, he hadn't even considered what the movie was so they'd sat down in a pair of recliners with a small table between, quickly loaded up with cheeseburgers, extra fries and a pair of Cokes bigger than his head, and watched the screen. It turned out to be a movie about a couple who banged...a lot. Sure they didn't show everything—it wasn't porn—and there was probably some other kind of plot to it, but all he could think about the whole time was how fucking hot it would be to reenact some of the scenes —especially the one where the guy fingered the girl to orgasm in a restaurant full of people and then had her suck his fingers clean.

His balls fucking ached. He snuck a quick glance at Tamara. Her gaze stayed on the screen as the credits rolled, her hands clasped in her lap and her back ramrod straight, which thrust her tits forward enough that he could make out how her hard nipples stood out firm against her clingy shirt. Was she turned on because of the movie or because she was thinking along the same lines as he was? Before he could decide, she stood up and smoothed her hands over her hips, easing her skirt back into place.

"Thank you again for helping me out," she said, each word enunciated a little too clearly. "But I'll get a cab from here back to my car."

"That's not smart with the bounty hunter still out there and you know it." Standing up, he took full advantage of the fact that he was tall enough at six feet, four inches to loom over her. "Come on, I'll give Marko a call. See if Wolczyk made a fuss at the party and we can figure out what happens next after that."

Her jaw tightened but she gave a small nod and started forward down the aisle. Letting his hand fall to the small of her back as they walked through the movie theater's exit was the gentlemanly thing to do. He'd had good home training. He knew the way to do things. That's all it was. It had nothing to do with giving in to the temptation to touch her and feel her move under his palm.

Your bullshit smells rank as carrion roasting on the highway, Camacho.

He helped her up into the truck before crossing around the cargo bed—scanning the area for movie-goers who looked a little too curious about them as he did—and sliding in behind the steering wheel. After a quick glance in the rearview mirror for anything out of place, his attention dropped to Tamara's reflection. Their gazes locked and he saw the same heated desire in her cool blue eyes as in his own. Subtlety wasn't his thing, didn't look like it was her either. They had that in common if nothing else.

"Your car's at the Corsair Club?" He turned the key in the ignition.

The question obviously caught her by surprise because she blinked a few times before looking away and answering. "The B-Squad garage. I caught a ride to the party."

"We'll head that way." He turned right out of the theater's parking lot and punched the Bluetooth connect button on the truck's steering wheel. "Call Mr. Chatty."

The phone rang twice before Marko Pike picked up. "Talk."

"Hello to you to," he drawled.

Silence filled the air, standard procedure for Marko, the B-Squad's demolitions expert who talked little and noticed everything.

Normally, Isaac would just let the dead air hang in an eternal test of wills between him and the closed-mouthed, muscle-bound enforcer. Today he didn't have the luxury of busting the other man's balls.

"Any excitement at the party?"

Marko snorted. "You mean besides you two sneaking off through the kitchen followed by an appearance by that jackass Wolczyk searching for someone named Tamara that none of us had seen in about a million years?"

"Where's he now?' Tamara asked, her voice tight.

"Poor guy tripped on his way out the door and messed up his wrist." Marko didn't sound the least bit sorry for the bounty hunter. Hell, he'd probably been the one to drop the guy. "He's at the ER getting it looked at."

She twisted the fabric in her skirt. "How do you know?"

"I have visual."

That was the B-Squad. They protected their own, even if the person in question had only recently joined their ranks.

Isaac turned onto the road leading to the Devil's Dip Gym building. It was half a city block big and held a below-ground secured parking garage, Taz's boxing gym on the main floor, and apartments for most of the team and the B-Squad headquarters. "Anything else I need to know?"

"Tons." Marko didn't elaborate.

Good thing Isaac didn't expect him to. "Good talk, Mr. Chatty."

"Fuck you." The line went dead.

"I've never heard Marko talk that much and I see him almost every day," Tamara said.

Isaac winked at her. "He likes me."

He pulled to a stop next to the keypad that would open the Devil's Dip Gym's private garage and entered his code and put his thumb against the fingerprint scanner. After a short beep, the garage door rolled up. Inside it was like a car fanatics' wet dream. If there was a high-end, tricked-out vehicle on the market—or about to enter it—the men and women of the B-Squad had it. It wasn't a cherry custom paint job or the enviable chrome work that identified what had to be Tamara's car. It was the beige, slightly dented ordinariness of it.

"A Camry?"

She shrugged. "I paid for it in cash and it gets the job done."

Taking in her designer dress that had a few well-repaired frays, he figured the past few months had been the first time in her adult life she'd had to settle for something that just 'got the job done.' He parked behind it, blocking her car in, then put his hand down on her seatbelt latch and covered it so she couldn't unbuckle.

He'd sit here all night like this if he had to but there was no way he could let her go back to that house until Wolczyk had moved on to search greener cases. The fact that Fane had called in a local, and not a very good one, as opposed to sending his own minions meant there might be hope that he thought finding Essie or Tamara in Fort Worth was a long shot.

"You can't go home tonight. If Wolczyk found you at the party, he could still show up at your house."

The stubborn tilt of her jaw said she wanted to argue and he braced himself.

"Fine," she said, obviously not happy about it. "I'll stay here."

Stubborn but not reckless. Now that was a mark in her favor. Not to mention smart. As far as crash pads went, she could do a helluva lot worse than a building that made Fort Knox look like an open house. Getting into the training gym was easy. Accessing any other part of the building without a key code and the right biometrics? Practically impossible. Plus, it was roomy as hell. When she'd designed her company headquarters, Bianca had made sure to keep a few rooms open for the occasional willing and not so willing overnight guest, so there was definitely space.

"You want me to take you home so you can grab some stuff?" he asked.

She gave him that fake beauty queen smile again. Either she knew it pushed him off kilter and liked doing it or she didn't give a fuck what it did to him. Even odds on either possibility.

"That's okay, I have a go-bag in my car." She snuck her fingers underneath his, sending a shock of electricity straight to his cock, then pressed the seatbelt latch release.

"Always prepared, huh?"

"You know us beauty queens." She opened the passenger door and stepped out onto the running board and then hopped off. "We need to be ready for any possibility."

He was out of his door in a flash and standing between her and the trunk of her car so nondescript it should belong to the Feds. "Like the Marines, just prettier and without the combat?"

"Oh honey, you've obviously never been backstage." She used her key fob to pop the trunk.

"Got rough did it?" The image of Tamara in her underwear and a white satin Miss Idaho sash in the middle of an all-female pillow fight flashed in his head.

Reaching around him, she snagged a hot pink duffle with a designer name stitched across the top from the trunk. "You do not want to know the damage boob tape or a few drops of sour flavoring in Vaseline can do."

"Vaseline?" He shut the trunk for her.

"You wear it to keep lipstick from getting on your teeth. If it tasted gross, you were stuck with that for the entire competition."

Now that was devious. "I think I'm starting to like you."

"You already did." She swapped her bag from her left to her right hand and shook out the fingers on her free hand and sat back against the closed trunk.

"Why is that, do you think?" He reached for the bag.

She didn't release her hold on it. "I have a vagina and from what I hear you like anyone with one of those."

Damn. He wasn't that bad. "Are you B-Squad ladies talking about me during your staff meetings?"

He maneuvered his body so he stood in front of her, his legs on either side of her, relishing the way her breath caught.

She didn't move away. "More like laughing."

But she wasn't now. Nope. A flush had spread from the V of her cleavage up to her very kissable full lips that were slightly parted and begging to be tasted. He dipped his head lower and rested his finger tips on her hips—not enough to hold her there but enough to let her know he wanted to.

He stopped close enough that there was nothing between them but sparks of anticipation. "Really?"

She opened her mouth to retort and he took full advantage of the moment. It wasn't a sweet kiss because neither of them had more than an ounce of sugar in them. They were determined, assertive, demanding people who took what they wanted—and this was their kind of kiss. They devoured each other. She tasted of white wine, salty fries and the kind of dick-hardening trouble that had pre-come pooling on the swollen tip of his cock. The second her tongue slid against his, teasing him just as much as turning him harder than a steel door, he would have given up his soul to find out just how far they could take this kiss—even in the Devil's Dip Gym garage that was outfitted with more surveillance cameras than the typical bank.

Let the B-Squad team watch. He just wanted to touch.

But that wasn't to be.

Way too soon, Tamara pressed a hand against his chest and pushed him back, taking away her sweet mouth and all the sinful possibilities there were in how he wanted to have her use it.

It was a toss-up on which ached more—his hard-on or his lungs as he tried to catch his breath.

For a second they just stared at each other, lips kiss-swollen and desire thick in their veins. Oh yes. She wanted him just as much as he wanted her. Whatever it was about blondes with bad attitudes that did him in, she obviously had the same thing for swaggering former Marines.

She was the first one to speak. "That's not happening again."

"Why not?" Because he wanted to do it again. Now. And more. So much more.

"I know all the blood in your brain hasn't gone south." She snuck under his arm that had been blocking her in place and strutted away, putting a few feet of daylight between them. "I've got a megalomaniacal cult leader on my tail because I'm hiding his daughter so he doesn't sell her off under the guise of a dutiful marriage. I don't have time or energy to get off on anything other than my own fingers right now."

Without giving him a chance to respond, she turned and walked toward the private elevator that would whisk her up to the B-Squad's main office. Her hips swayed a little more than normal as she strutted across the garage, her heels clicking on the pristine cement floor. The elevator opened as soon as she put her thumb on the scanner and she strolled inside.

He waited for the doors to close before taking his phone out of his front jeans pocket, a process made more difficult by the fact that his pants were a lot tighter than they'd been before he'd kissed Tamara. He hit the first contact number.

"Lash. Give me Tamara's home address. I need to go do a sweep and double-check your work, slackass."

Tamara

Tamara's palms were sweaty, her hair messed up, her pulse erratic and her hormones way out of control. As the elevator zipped up to B-Squad's headquarters on the second floor, she wiped her palms on her skirt, smoothed her hair, and told her hormones to shut the fuck up. She hadn't been lying to Isaac. She did not have time for romance of even the one-night, multiple-orgasm, boneless-satisfaction variety. By the time the elevator doors opened, she was back to her natural impermeable state of being.

Marching across the lobby and heading straight for her office, she laid out her priorities in a mental checklist. First, she needed to figure out how to touch base with Essie in Colorado without leading Jarrod and his bounty hunter straight to the teen who had a Mensa-sized brain and whose first taste of freedom outside her father's compound was inching toward the wild side. If it wasn't for the fact that her former beauty pageant mentor Albert Glad-Lovatt was keeping a close eye on the sixteen-year-old. The man had kept Tamara in line. Essie would be a cake walk.

Second, she had to find out how Archie Wolczyk had tracked her to the engagement party. Isaac was right. God, that sucked to even think silently to herself. Her house had to be off- limits until further notice. Her office had a couch that would work out perfectly. No one on the team would need to know that she was crashing here for a few days until things cooled down. The last thing she wanted—or needed—was to give Bianca an excuse to rethink hiring her after all Tamara had done to fuck things up between her new boss and her ex-husband.

"Going somewhere, or planning to haul out someone's head?"

Shit.

Tamara jerked to a stop. She schooled her face into a neutral mask before turning and greeting the brunette staring daggers at her. "Hi there."

Elisa Sharp leaned against the doorway of her office directly across from Tamara's. Elisa, the team's resident transformation artist and the daughter of one of Texas's most notorious con artists, was one of the last people Tamara wanted to run into right now. The woman could smell a lie a mile away and detect an evasion from space. It was what made her so damned good at her job—and not just a little bit scary.

"I'm couch-surfing here for a couple of days." Okay, that was the truth. Not all of it, but enough to pass the human lie detector.

Elisa didn't blink. "What's wrong with your place?"

She wasn't ready for a follow up and blurted out the first thing that came to mind. "An infestation."

"Of the bounty-hunter phylum?" Elisa strolled out into the hall in that controlled, predatory way of hers with her head cocked to the left as she eyeballed Tamara. "Wanted for breaking and entering, not to mention kidnapping? You didn't tell us the law was after you when you hightailed it out of Idaho with your niece to escape her dad."

When would she learn? The truth always caught up with her in the end.

"Taz and Bianca knew." She let the heavy go-bag drop to the floor as she stood in the doorway to her office. "It's not what it looks like."

"That's disappointing. Rescuing your niece from a David Koresh wanna-be seemed pretty badass to me."

Tamara didn't know what to do with that—compliments that weren't related to how she looked were as foreign as Jupiter—so she ignored it. "I need to call Essie and warn her."

"And your phone isn't going to work."

For once, Tamara appreciated the other woman's ability to ferret out the unspoken details that mattered.

"It's not in my name, but I can't take the chance that Wolczyk is running the numbers of the phones used to call or be called by the B-Squad office. My number is on that list about a billion times. It'll stick out like a sore thumb. I could lead Jarrod to Essie."

The other woman walked over to the supply alcove filled with the regular office must-haves along with the items unique to an organization like the B-Squad.

"What you need is a burner." Elisa swiped one of several phones and held it out to Tamara. "Here."

"I can't use this." She gulped. She was only here until Essie's eighteenth birthday. After that Essie would be safe from the threat of Jarrod winning custody of her. Tamara knew she didn't belong. She wasn't part of the team. "They're B-Squad's."

A rare smile instead of Elisa's usual smirk. "So are you."

Again, there were no words, so she took the phone. As the other woman retreated into her office, Tamara called the number she'd memorized but had never written down. It rang once. She hung up and dialed again. This time she held on for two rings before disconnecting. She punched in the number a third time. One ring. Two rings.

It stopped ringing.

Her heart climbed up into her throat.

"Hey Aunt T." Essie's chipper almost-a-grown-up voice came over the line. "What's up?"

The breath she'd been holding escaped and her internal organs shifted back into their normal position. "You answered without waiting for the special ring."

"You're paranoid," she said in the dismissive know-it-all way that was the hallmark of every teenager, and with one as smart as Essie it was even worse.

Tamara pinched the bridge of her nose to ease the rush of loving frustration steaming her from the inside out. "No. I'm not. There was a bounty hunter here today. That means your dad hasn't given up."

Dead air.

Finally, Essie let out a loud breath. "Shit."

She winced at the word. "Don't use that language." Not because she thought it was out of bounds but because her sister Amelia had always been so proper and restrained. She'd never cursed, not even when she'd been diagnosed with late-stage ovarian cancer. The least Tamara could do is keep her niece from sounding like a longshoreman. "And yes, shit."

"So I guess you weren't being overly cautious when you went back to Texas instead of staying here with me in Colorado."

That had hurt, like gnawing-off-your-own-limb pain, but Jarrod's only tie to Essie's location was Tamara and she couldn't be the weak link. Not again. This time she was taking her sister's advice. "Layers. It's important to have layers of safety."

"Okay, I get it."

The sad note in Essie's voice gutted Tamara. She'd give anything in the world to change it, but the truth was she couldn't. She didn't have the money to fight Jarrod in court even if he didn't have the local judges in his pocket. If only she'd put away some of her gold-digging profits instead of spending them on stupid shit like her hot pink overnighter. She kicked the bag hard enough that it slid under her desk.

"Es, we should be okay, but be on the lookout."

"Always. I'm like an owl on Ritalin."

Tamara stifled her chuckle at the image. "Don't let down your guard."

"You worry too much."

"That's not even possible." She stopped in front of the picture on her desk showing Amelia holding baby Essie with the sun streaming down on both of them. It was the only personal memento in her office or the tiny house on Philbert Street. "Love you Essie. Stay safe and give Albert my love."

"Ditto, Aunt T."

She hung up and tossed the burner phone onto the couch that would be her bed for the next few days. It was lumpy and too short for her, but it was better than the alternative. A few nights of crappy sleep was more than worth avoiding the bounty hunter or one of Jarrod's paid henchmen. No matter what it took or what she had to do, she would make sure Jarrod never got his hands on Essie again.

CHAPTER THREE

Isaac

The next day, Isaac scanned the Devil's Dip Gym looking for anyone or anything that seemed shady. Considering this was a functioning boxing gym and the fighters training in the ring and pounding the heavy bags weren't weekend warriors but the real deal, that meant there were plenty of shady characters around, from the wanna-be managers to the less than ethical promoters.

This was going to be like hunting black cats at midnight on a moonless night. Either Wolczyk was shooting darts blindfolded and was following up at Tamara's ex-husband's place because he really didn't know she was in Fort Worth, or someone here had tipped off the piss-poor bounty hunter. God knew there were plenty of Chatty Cathys around the gym. Old ladies at a coffee klatch had nothing on fighters when it came to gossiping.

"This is fucking ridiculous," he grumbled to Lash Finch as the other man handed him a mug of coffee strong enough to put fur on one of those ugly-ass hairless cats.

"What?" Lash asked with a shit-eating grin. "Your hard-on for Tamara or the amount of product in your hair to give it that girly shine you love."

Let a buddy crash at your place one time after a drunken week of booze and blondes in Cabo—not to mention a pair of beautiful brunettes—and deal with shit for a lifetime.

Isaac flipped him off. "The fact that Taz still has this gym open to anyone who strolls in."

"You got something against boxing all of a sudden?"

"With everything that's going on upstairs? Yeah, I do." Any one of these fools could endanger Tamara with a single mention to the wrong person—

and a sexy woman like her got noticed and talked about.

"The B-Squad floors are secure and Taz likes keeping this place open to up-and-coming fighters. It reminds him of Freddie." Lash's jaw hardened. "Shit, it reminds all of us of him."

Seventeen years ago, Freddie Atlas had caught Lash, Marko and Taz along with the rest of their boyhood crew and current B-Squad team members, Duke and Keir, breaking into the Devil's Dip Gym. Instead of turning the band of juvenile delinquents in to the cops, he'd taken them under his wing and trained them to be fighters. Taz had gone pro, making it all the way to the championship match. The other four had joined the military. After Freddie had died, the five of them made their way back to Fort Worth and the Devil's Dip Gym they all called home now. Isaac understood the connection and the meaning behind the gym even if he still thought it was crazy.

The front doors opened and Marko strolled in, looking like he could clean the floor with even the largest guy in the ring without breaking a sweat. Big didn't cover it. Snarly attitude didn't cover it. He looked like he kicked ass for a living and picked his teeth with the bones of his enemies. The fact that he glowered more than talked only enhanced the image.

"Morning, Mr. Chatty."

Marko jerked his chin in acknowledgement.

"What's the latest on Wolczyk?" Isaac asked.

"Sitting on his brains out front," Marko responded.

The urge to punch the mere idea of Tamara out of the bounty hunter's head had him fisting his hands. "Are you shitting me?" Isaac turned toward the door, but two heavy hands clamped down on his shoulders in mid-spin.

When he stopped moving he was almost nose to nose with one of his oldest friends and the best guy he could ever have next to him in a foxhole.

"Stop leading with your dick and your ego," Lash said, all the normal easy-going bullshitting charm draining right out of his voice. "You're not a one-man super show. We got this."

He thrust his forearms up and broke the other man's old. "How's that?"

"We'll let Wolczyk stew out front with his crappy cup of overpriced coffee and his talk radio, then go feed him some bullshit about Tamara's location," he said. "He can pass that news onto his client and then return to his normal routine of following cheating spouses."

Even through the misty red haze, he had to admit it wasn't a bad plan, but they were forgetting one thing. He shot a hard look at Marko. "Wolczyk's gotta still be pissed at you after his trip and fall at the club yesterday. He'll disregard any info you give him. I'll do it."

"You're not B-Squad, as you're so fond of telling us all the damn time," Lash said. "Why do you care so much?"

It was a question he didn't want to answer. "I don't care."

Marko snorted. "I think he has feelings. The kind that go straight to his sad excuse of a dick."

"Your mom doesn't complain," Isaac quipped.

Lash gave him a shove toward the door before Marko could deliver a harder one of his own. For such a bear of a man, Marko was a total softie when it came to his mom, which meant Isaac could never resist a good Yo Mama barb.

The perfectly delivered insult evened his nerves out and Isaac pushed his way through the front door and out into the bright Texas sunshine. It only took him a second to identify Wolczyk's car. In the land of pickup trucks, the bounty hunter drove a Prius. It was enough to make the great state of Texas weep. He hustled across the street and tapped on the driver's side window.

The other man didn't bother to glance his way as he rolled down the window. The smell of patchouli and sound of New Age music wafted out of the car.

"Camacho."

"Heard you're looking for Taz's ex-wife."

"Yeah." His gaze bounced from the gym's front door to Isaac.

"What makes you think she's in Fort Worth?"

The bounty hunter shrugged. "I don't."

"Why not?" Isaac played along. He may not be Elisa, but he knew how to run a simple con. "Who wouldn't want to be in Texas?"

"This chick. She's all high-maintenance and gold digging. She's probably on the hunt for her next marital conquest, poor rich bastard."

Isaac let Wolczyk's last words hang in the air between them. The man was a talker. He'd break down. His type always did.

He didn't have to wait long.

"So this guy in Idaho who employed me has hired investigators all over the country—anywhere this Tamara woman had ties. There's no rhyme or reason to it beyond that if you ask me. The guy is grasping at straws. In the meantime my ass is growing an ass while I keep surveillance on this place."

"I can help there. While I was inside, Taz got a call from someone named Tamara in Connecticut."

"Really? Why share that with me?"

"Because it's no skin off my nose and Taz doesn't give two shits about his ex. But if you'd rather spend the next few days watching the Devil's Dip Gym building in hopes of seeing someone who's not there, be my guest."

"Fuck that." Wolczyk turned the key in the ignition that didn't even make a single purr. "I owe you one, Camacho."

He tapped the roof of the Prius and took a step away before it silently drove down the block and turned at the corner. Wolczyk was gone—for the moment. The guy wasn't a great investigator, but he was just good enough to be a pain in the ass. Good thing Isaac excelled at distraction and protection—along with general badassery.

He pulled out his phone and hit the first contact on his list.

"What? Do you want me to massage your massive ego now?" Lash asked.

"Meet me at Tamara's." He crossed the street to his truck parked on the street. "Her security is about to get an upgrade."

The mother of all upgrades, to be more specific. No one was going to get within a block of Tamara's house without him knowing about it.

CHAPTER FOUR

Tamara

Two days later and all Tamara had to show for her amateur sleuthing debut was a permanent crick in her neck from her lumpy office couch and a whole lotta nothing on how Archie Wolczyk had stumbled upon her. After her research into the myriad of complaints against the bounty hunter at the Better Business Bureau, she was beyond convinced that that would be the only way he'd found her. The man bumbled more than a fat bee high on pollen.

Still, she wasn't doing much better, which was why she was pacing the main hallway of B-Squad HQ. Her office was awesome, but it was definitely getting that whole lived-in vibe and the walls were starting to close in on her. Playing it safe was starting to make her nuts. Well, that and the fact that Isaac Camacho kept popping up in her thoughts and in real life enough that everyone on the B-Squad was starting to make comments. The reminder of the evil that people could do was enough to drag her back to what mattered; not the pain in her neck or the cabin fever, but keeping Jarrod away from Essie. For that, she could endure whatever it took. Tolerating the danger wasn't enough though. She had to make sure that the bounty hunter was really as out of her life as it seemed before she could go home again and figure out whether Essie was safe in Colorado or if it was time to relocate.

Stopping in front of the wall of video screens in the hall outside her office, she scanned the twenty-three different views of the Devil's Dip Gym building, both inside and out. No Prius matching the one registered to Archie Wolczyk on the street. No bounty hunter hanging around. He'd driven off forty-eight hours ago after a car-side conference with Isaac—

wouldn't she just love to know what that little tit for tat had been about—and hadn't been seen since.

"Isn't that sweet, you just couldn't wait for me to get here today could you?" Isaac's voice boomed across the empty space between the elevator and the monitors that she knew was anything but unobserved.

Oh no. Ever since she'd hightailed it out of Taz's and Bianca's engagement party, everyone in the office seemed to be keeping tabs on her and tracking just how much the freelance investigator had been appearing at the B-Squad's headquarters. She'd barely noticed, of course. Isaac Camacho and his overabundance of sex appeal was just another thing she didn't have time for.

So why is you belly doing that triple-flip thing as you watch that handsome hunk of hotness in tight jeans head straight toward you?

Stapling her inner hussy's lips shut, she forced her gaze back to the monitors. "I suppose you're just in the neighborhood. Again."

"Something like that. I come bearing churros." He held up a brown paper bag, drawing her attention back where it had no business being. "They're still hot from my kitchen."

God save her thighs. Living a life of culinary denial for the past thirty years had given her a sweet tooth that couldn't be denied—just the kind of thing that called for friend dough rolled in cinnamon sugar.

Sure. Blame your fascination on the churros. Not Isaac's biceps and pecs shown off to perfection in a black T-shirt or his confident strut or his tempting mouth that you imagined all over you while you circled your clit until you came last night.

"You made them?" Yeah, more like someone angling for a second night over at Casa Camacho had whipped them up while probably naked except for a frilly pink apron.

Not liking the sizzle of jealousy that thought caused, she turned and headed back down the hall toward her office and away from the man who seemed determined to drag her off task.

"You doubt my prowess?" he asked, ignoring her brush off and following a few steps behind her.

"In the kitchen?" she scoffed.

"Trust me, darlin', I've got skills for every room in the house. Your kitchen, however, has shoes in the stove."

She jerked to a stop just inside her office and spun around to face him, heat beating at her cheeks. "What do you mean my kitchen? What were you doing in my house?"

The smug bastard didn't even have the smarts to look embarrassed. He looked pleased. And like everything else, it looked good on him. It wasn't fair.

"I was beefing up Lash's security measures." He leaned one broad shoulder against the doorjamb and crossed one booted foot over the other

—the picture of a man at home no matter where he was. "It seems you weren't exactly honest with him about your needs in that department."

Pushing away any question of what it would be like to be that comfortable anywhere while buying herself some time to figure out what to say next, she walked to her desk and sat down. Her heart was still hammering, but she didn't have to worry about her shaking knees giving her away once she was settled in behind her desk. Sitting in the ergonomically adjusted chair, she opened her laptop with its alphabetically organized virtual folders and color-coded email notification system. Happiness was a perfectly organized desktop and brand new Manolos on her feet. She had one, if not the other, and she'd learned to accept that. Her life had taken a left turn from being all about getting what she wanted to doing what she needed the moment her sister expended her last breath on asking Tamara to keep Essie safe. It was the only thing that mattered.

She logged in to her laptop, but Isaac didn't go away. He just stood there sucking up all the oxygen in the room and making her pulse erratic. The stubborn jackass obviously wasn't going anywhere until he got the answer to his unasked question.

"I told Lash what he needed to know." She scrolled through her email, fighting the instinct to look up at Isaac and drink in every detail about him from the scuffed toe on his right boot to the way his jeans rode low on his hips to the smug grin on his lips that she wanted desperately to either slap off or kiss off—it was a toss-up which would eventually happen.

Isaac didn't take the unspoken but clearly telegraphed hint to skedaddle. He strolled deeper into her office, stopping in front of the photo of her sister with baby Essie, and picked it up. The way he looked at it made it seem as if he could see more than what was there in front of him in black and white—as if he wanted to get a peek at what was below the surface to whatever was real and raw and true. Maybe he could see the light in Amelia —her sister always had it—but he sure as hell wasn't going to get a good look at what was underneath Tamara's icy facade.

No one knew the importance of keeping up appearances better than Tamara. What was it her mother had always said? Oh yes. Don't let them see the ugly until you've already talked them out of a prenup and the ring's on your finger. It was the only way, her mother had warned again and again and again until it had been imprinted on Tamara's brain, to prepare for the inevitable day when her looks faded and her rich husband realized there was nothing else to her but sagging tits and a fast-widening ass.

You've got exactly one thing going for you, Tamara Anne—and the clock started ticking on it the second you got your first period.

There was nothing quite like her mother's loving pep talks.

"For someone who hates being in the dark, you sure do tend to leave others playing guessing games." Isaac sat the photo down with a reverent gentleness and turned to her, something serious lurking in his gaze. "That'll catch up to you one of these days."

Shoving the rest of her mom's little gems of advice back into a deep, dark mental hole, she started typing an email composed of total gibberish. "Well, that's not something you ever have to worry about."

"But I do, because I spend hours just wondering about you." His large shadow fell across her keyboard. "So tell me, Tamara darlin', what other needs can I help you take care of?"

Her fingers faltered on the keyboard before speeding up. "You could help with my need for quiet by leaving."

"I'm wounded." He slapped his palm onto his muscular chest. "And after all I've done to make that messy little bungalow of yours safe enough so you could go home without worry."

Despite her best intentions, a sense of gratefulness settled in her belly like an unfamiliar snack. "I never asked you to."

"That's alright, you can thank me over dinner. What night this week are you free?"

No matter how tempting it was to follow up that kiss in the garage with a hard, slow, and thorough fuck, she didn't have that option. Like every other luxury in her life, the ability to let down her guard with anyone was a thing of the past.

"Let me see." She clicked on her calendar, picked a date and started typing. "Here we go."

Keeping her chin at the perfect haughty level and her gaze as uninterested as possible considering the circumstances, she turned her laptop around so he could read what she'd typed.

WHEN HELL FREEZES OVER.

Isaac grinned, one corner of his mouth pulling up higher than the other in a way that should have made him look goofy.Instead, it just made her grateful she was sitting down and wearing panties for once. Her five-season-old Diane Von Furstenberg wrap dress had been through enough already without having to deal with her very physical reaction to him. His gaze dropped to her peaked nipples poking at the silk jersey material as she internally cursed her choice in bras this morning. Where were the obnoxiously padded Victoria's Secret bras when she needed one?

"I see you can already feel it. There's definitely a chill in the air already." The bastard winked at her and dropped the churro bag on her keyboard. "See ya soon."

Watching him strut out of her office was good for many reasons, but number one because her sanity started to resurface. It definitely wasn't because of the perfect view of his tight ass. Nope. Not at all.

She was still staring at the empty doorway, mouth slightly agape, a minute later when Elisa, Vivi and Lexie walked through it. As always, Vivi strode in like the world was hers—definitely a holdover from her DEA agent days. Lexie strolled in behind her, typing away on her tablet—no doubt hacking into one database or another, wearing a T-shirt that declared I PET MY PUSSY EVERY DAY over a screen-printed picture of her cat, Ruffles. As always, Elisa hung back, observing the terrain before taking a step in side and stationing herself by the door for a fast get away.

Lexie tossed her tablet onto Tamara's office couch and grabbed the churro bag, then opened it and took a deep inhale. Bleached blonde with tattoos from the spot behind her ear to her toes and ever-present cherry red lipstick (which she called the blood of her enemies), Lexie had never looked as angelically happy as she did when she pulled out a churro and took a bite.

"Isaac might feel a chill but I'm getting fucking hot and bothered and he's not even flirting with me." Lexie took another bite, her eyes fluttering shut for a second before snapping back open. "Will you please sleep with him so the churros continue? Think of your friends. We have needs. Sugary. Cinnamony. Fried Doughy. Needs."

Of course they'd been eavesdropping. Why had she ever thought they wouldn't be?

Vivi hooked a finger in the bag and glanced inside but wisely didn't try to claim it. "I don't even like churros and I'd fuck that boy silly."

"So when are you going to say yes?" Elisa asked from her spot by the door. "We have an office pool going."

She shrugged. "I'm not."

The other three women started laughing in disbelief, Vivi so hard she snorted. Tamara didn't mean to join in, but the laughter bubbled up inside her and she snagged the bag of churros before Lexie could inhale them all.

It was ridiculous. She wasn't sleeping with Isaac Camacho. Even if she had time for a man, he wasn't her type, which was rich, CEOs on the hunt for a trophy wife who rarely, if ever, made her lungs tighten with anticipation or her legs wobbly with want. Only trouble lay that way, and she had more than enough of that in her life already.

CHAPTER FIVE

Isaac

Isaac hadn't whacked off in the shower so much since he'd first started getting boners.

Masturbation wasn't exactly the thing he should be thinking about the day after Tamara had turned him down for a date again...but it was. Like an asshole, he couldn't stop thinking about how badly he wanted to fuck her—no, like a dammed sap he couldn't stop thinking about her, just her—even as he stood in the middle of the Devil's Dip Gym filled as usual with sweaty, young fighters determined to prove themselves, grizzled trainers, and managers with dollar signs in their eyes.

He gave each one a hard look, but no one set off his danger detector. Lash and Keir Locke, B-Squad's resident fixer, had gone through the building's closed-circuit video streams, phone records, and anything else that might tip them off about how Wolczyk had gotten turned on to the possibility Tamara was hiding out under the B-Squad umbrella. She was Taz's ex-wife, so it made sense to check the place out, but the question was, had the bounty hunter almost clapped eyes on her because of dumb luck or something else?

Before he could complete a second scan of the room, Kelvin Park stepped into his field of vision—at least the bottom half of it. Kelvin may have been as muscled and tough as a cornered bull hopped up on meth and tequila, but at five feet, eight inches tall, he wasn't coming close to blocking out Isaac's view of the possible suspects.

"You again?" The gym manager pivoted to stand beside Isaac and then held out a Styrofoam cup of sludge with delusions of being coffee.

"Keeping track of me? I'm touched." He accepted the cup and shot back a mouthful of lukewarm liquid.

It was strong enough to make his eyes water and his chest sprout new hair. Whatever Park was putting in the coffee pot it shouldn't be given to small children or the mentally unbalanced.

The other man snorted. "More like wondering why in the fuck you're repeatedly showing up here like head lice in a pre-school."

"Sage got sent home again?"

Kelvin had more war stories from being a single parent to a four-year-old princess in training than the grizzliest Recon staff sergeant. The latest all centered around the Battle of Head Lice Hill. Listening to his stories had Isaac's whole body itching.

"That shit is the plague." The gym manager scratched the back of his skull, caught himself in mid-itch and groaned. "It's starting to mess with my head."

"Mayonnaise." He gripped the cup tighter to keep from scratching the sudden phantom itch, cracking the Styrofoam and soaking his hand before he could drop it in the trash can next to Kelvin's desk near the gym's front door. "Slick it on there, have her sleep in a shower cap and suffocate the suckers."

One eyebrow raise was all it took for the other man to signal that he hadn't missed that overreaction. "And exactly how do you know this?"

"Five sisters. All younger. Single mom." He took a towel off the stack on the corner of Kelvin's desk in easy grab-and-go reach for the occasional blood-spurting nose after a hard hit and wiped the coffee off his hand. "There was no such thing as 'not my problem' in our house."

A quick flick of his wrist and the towel landed in the canvas laundry bag on the floor. Oh yes, he'd been house trained and then some. He knew when to come armed with chocolate and when retreat was the only option —something that had saved him more than once when it came to the women he loved and the ones he only loved for a night.

In the ring, two fighters switched from silent sparring to shoving and hurling curses at each other. The light heavyweight in green shorts got out something about the other fighter's mom and donkey dick when a trainer stepped between them. Neither fighter looked ready to let go, though. Park barked out an order for the two smack-talking idiots to cut the shit and they backed off. Proof that when it came to brawling, testosterone had nothing on estrogen—even the pip-squeak variety.

After a shouted snarl that heads mattered more in a match than fists, Kelvin turned back to Isaac. "It really works?"

He nodded as he scanned the gym for unfamiliar faces. "Anyone new hanging out here lately?"

"I'll give you the same answer as I gave you yesterday and the day before and the day before that. No."

Not that he'd been expecting anything different, but a break would be nice. Until he could nail down who had tipped off Wolczyk about the party, he wouldn't be able to determine if she was still in danger from Fane and his shitballs-crazy cult members. "No one asking about Tamara?"

"People mostly keep to themselves. They don't chat. It's a gym, not a women's bathroom."

He cut a glance at the other man. They both knew that was some high-frequency bullshit. A gym was guaranteed to be filled with the stink of sweat and gossip about who was doing what, who, and when.

"Anyone acting weird?" he asked.

"Besides you and that one there—who has every fucking reason in the world to spend hours every day pounding the shit out of that heavy bag?" Kelvin nodded toward Gidget Harms, grim-faced and dead-eyed, pummeling the black and red bag chained to a support beam. "Not any more than normal. You gotta be at least a little crazy to want to step into the ring and face off against someone who wants to beat your head in. It's almost as bad as those poor idiots who keep circling around the same woman who doesn't have one little bit of interest in him." He didn't bother to smother his smirk. "Not that you know what that's like."

The man had the subtlety of a two-by-four studded with nails. "You're a fucking riot, Kelvin."

He just grinned. "That's what they say."

Refusing to cop to the inner voice echoing everything Kelvin was goading him about, the guy code mandated that he couldn't leave without delivering one last little verbal love tap. "Good luck with the lice. If your head starts itching, don't wait to check it out. Those suckers love to jump from one head to the other. Makes me itchy just thinking about it."

"You're a real dick, Camacho." Kelvin flipped him off.

He returned the non-verbal endearment. "That's what they say."

As he made his way past the main sparring ring, the speed bags, and the fighters practicing footwork in front of the mirrors, he took narrowed down approaches to get the most information possible out of Gidget. The woman was on the thin edge and was just as likely to jump the line as she was to stay sane. Not that anyone could expect her to be any different. It had only been a few months since the B-Squad had rescued her from a whack job on the DEA's Top Ten. Yasmin Romanow had a personal grudge against the women of the B-Squad and had kidnapped Gidget and then used her as a human guinea pig for six months, testing out the mind-control drug Genie's Wish. During the rescue op, Bianca had gotten drugged and nearly killed Taz on Romanow's orders. The whole thing had nearly gone down in a ball of flames, but the team had managed to make it out and saved Gidget. She'd come home physically unharmed, but hurt in a whole other way.

He hadn't known her before she'd been kidnapped. From what he could gather, she'd been just another carefree, rich party girl without a single person in the world who cared for her besides Bianca, Vivi, Lexi and Elisa —her girls from St. Bernadette's Academy for Young Ladies, a sort of reform school for rich girls gone bad. They'd been the ones determined to find her, but the woman they'd brought back wasn't the one they'd known from before. An air of angry fragility hung over her, but he couldn't help but think there was more strength inside her than she let show. No one could have survived what she had without it.

Giving the heavy bag one last punch, she turned as he approached and sat down on the wooden bench in front of the lockers. Bright red hair pulled back into a tight ponytail, pale skin pink with exertion, and sweat turning her oversized gray T-shirt black in spots, she kept her gaze on the men sparring in the ring instead of Isaac who stood in front of her.

Okay. This was going to go well, he could just tell. "Hi Gidget."

Her gaze flickered over to him for half a second before snapping back to the fighters.

Strike one. Good thing he didn't give up easy.

"You down here every day?"

Acting like he wasn't even there talking to her, Gidget lifted her right wrist to her mouth, took the Velcro flap of her training glove between her teeth and yanked it open.

Strike two. Way to suck wind, Camacho.

"Have you noticed anyone out of place? Heard of anyone asking about Tamara? Know of anybody who knew the B-Squad would be gathered at the engagement party?"

Gidget trained her focus on him, but didn't say a word. She just went to work on her other glove.

Okay, she was looking at him. Glaring. Snarling a little. But there was eye contact. That was progress, right? Shoving back the annoyance at the lack of answers from anyone about how Wolczyk knew to show up at Taz's and Bianca's engagement party, he pushed forward. Interrogation wasn't his thing—his patience was for shit—but he refused to give up.

"Look, Tamara's hiding for a damn good reason, but the asshole found her anyway. I've got to figure out how before he realizes he hit the jackpot and comes after her."

Her only response was to pull off both gloves and reach for the water bottle next to her on the bench. She took a long drink then stood up as if he hadn't been there at all and headed for the locker room. It was enough to shred the last frayed thread of patience. Without thinking it through, he grabbed Gidget's elbow and stopped her in mid-step.

"There's a good chance her life—and that of a sixteen year old girl—is at stake if he finds them. If you know anything that might help..."

He followed her gaze down to his hand on her arm. Shame, cold and heavy, sank down on him and he let go. Neither of them moved. The request hung in the air for a second before crashing to the ground and imploding upon impact.

"Gidget, I'm sorry. I didn't mean—" He fumbled for a proper apology. "I know you've been through a lot and I shouldn't have—"

"Green shorts," she said, her voice raspy and low.

His brain tried to catch the secret meaning behind her first words. "What?"

"Getting out of the ring now. He earns extra cash running errands for Bianca. He helped run things over to Corsair Club for the engagement party."

Fuck. Here he was stuck in his own head when he should have been thinking about what was going on in hers. You're a real asshole, Camacho.

"Thanks, Gidget."

She dipped her chin in a sharp nod. "Don't let them get her."

Then without another word, she tucked her arm in close to her side to avoid touching him and walked past him to the locker room.

He pivoted to get a look at the fighter in the green shorts who'd just taken off the padded face protection Kelvin insisted fighters wear when sparring. The kid was young, with an eager face and a cocky grin. That wasn't what set off Isaac's danger alert though—it was the woman strutting across the gym in high heels and an ass-hugging blue skirt that made his cock immediately stand up and say hello.

What in the hell was Tamara Post doing downstairs in the Devil's Dip Gym?

As if his gaze had weight, she brought her hand to her cheek and turned. The second she spotted him, her blue eyes narrowed and she made a sharp turn to come straight at him. Fuck. She was a sight to behold. The ice queen melted a little more each time they met. Pretty soon she'd be blazing and he couldn't wait for that. He had every intention of going up in flames with her.

She stopped in front of him, exasperation—and maybe a little of something else—turning her cheeks pink. "What are you doing here?"

"I could ask you the same thing." Because she had no business being in anon-secure location until they knew for sure that Wolczyk had given up on her being in Fort Worth and reported that misinformation back to Fane.

"I work here."

"Oh really?" He asked, letting some of his own frustration—about her safety and otherwise—leak into his tone. "Are you picking up some extra hours in the gym? Looking for a sparring partner?"

There is was. That spark of something extra chipping away at her frozen exterior. But the moment he spotted it, she managed to transform her features into that damned frosty mask of hers that didn't give away a thing about the woman hiding behind it. Instead of fiery, her gaze turned bored. Instead of a heated flush in her cheeks, she lifted her chin a few haughty inches. Tamara was gone and the impenetrable ice queen back in place.

Without another word, she turned and sauntered over to the ring where the fighter in the green shorts was downing a bottle of water.

"Bryson." The smile she gave him was anything but glacial. It was downright friendly. "You helped out Bianca with the engagement party right?"

The fighter nodded his head, a cocky grin on his face like he even stood a chance. "Yeah, I took the centerpieces over for her."

"Did you get anyone to help you carry it out?" Tamara asked.

Isaac knew exactly where she was going with this. Looked like someone had been busy while under lockdown in the B-Squad offices. He had to admire her determination to be in control of her own destiny, even as he realized it was going to make keeping her safe that much harder.

"Nah." The fighter flexed like only an idiot twenty-year-old did in front of a hot chick. "I can carry a lot more than a couple of boxes. If it wasn't for forgetting to take my keys out of my pocket before I went outside I would've been able to get them into the car on my own too."

Tamara tensed. It was just the slightest tightness in her jaw and it disappeared almost immediately, but he caught it. The urge to pounce on the kid and shake him until all the details rolled out had Isaac by the balls, but he resisted. Tamara was working her source like a pro. If he didn't know better, he'd think she was a B-Squad agent instead of the office manager.

"What happened?" she asked.

"Dude got out of a Prius and held the boxes while I got my keys out." The utterly-clueless-and-in-need-of-a- smack-to-the-head Bryson said. "They didn't get messed up did they?"

"No." Tamara patted the fighter's forearm.

It was a reassuring gesture to keep Bryson talking, but the interrogator's trick had the opposite effect on Isaac. Jealousy—cold, hard and solid—hit him straight in the gut, as unusual as it was tangible.

"They were perfect," she continued. "Did you happen to tell him where you were delivering the centerpieces?"

Bryson dropped his attention from the sexy woman in front of him to the tip of his left shoe. "I might have."

'Might have' his ass. The kid had given up the location of the party. Time for good cop to give way to pissed off cop. The kid was a contender, but Isaac was bigger, meaner and more experienced in the ways of scaring the shit out of young punks.

He slipped between Tamara and Bryson. "Did you or didn't you?"

"Yeah," he squeaked out. "He said he wanted to talk to Mr. Hazard in a neutral location. I know you guys are working cases upstairs. I figured he wanted to share information without looking like a snitch." He made a half-hearted kick at the gym's concrete floor. "I should have told someone. I'm really sorry."

Tamara's pointed elbow landed firmly between two of Isaac's rib as she circled around him to face the fighter. "Don't worry about it, Bryson. You didn't do anything wrong."

The other man mumbled a thanks and hustled off to the locker room, leaving Tamara in all of her icy glory standing next to him.

"There was no need to go all asshole on him," she said as she examined her red nails. "He didn't do anything wrong."

For once when he was around Tamara, Isaac's brain got the upper hand over his dick. The moron had leaked the party location. That he didn't realize he was doing anything wrong was beside the point. He could have gotten Tamara killed. There wasn't a single shred of a doubt in his mind that Fane wouldn't bypass any kind of legal processing and skip straight to doing whatever it took to get Essie's location out of Tamara—even if that meant having to do a very final clean up afterward so no one would ever know what happened. Keir had put together a complete brief on the cult leader. Fane didn't think he was above the law. He thought he was the law.

"He didn't do anything wrong?" He shoved his fingers through his hair hard enough to yank a few out. "He gave you up to Wolczyk."

She shrugged. "It was an accident."

"The kind that could've given Fane your location," he bit out.

He didn't need to elaborate the world of hurt that would come down after Fane found her so the bastard could peel Essie's location out of Tamara's brain. She knew. The truth was written in the pinched tightness around her eyes and the sudden pallor on her skin.

"But it didn't." She brushed her hands across the swell of her hips and threw back her shoulders while a dangerous gleam blazed in her blue eyes.

Oh shit. "I know that look."

"What look is that?" For the first time since she clamped eyes on Bryson, she turned her full attention to Isaac.

Something shifted inside him as his cock tried to take the wheel from his brain. Exactly the effect she knew she'd have on him. He had to hand it to her, the woman used ever tool at her disposal to get her way—and that meant turning him into a horny idiot who'd get the hell out of her way. If he wasn't so familiar from using the same tactic himself, he'd be pissed off. As it was, he had to admire her commitment. Too bad it wasn't gonna work.

"The one that says you're already planning to run."

Her gaze held steady, but clasped her hands together tight enough to turn her knuckles white. "That's not the word I'd choose."

"Semantics."

"Call it what you want then, just keep your mouth shut about it." The mask dropped and she showed off her true glory. She wasn't an avenging angel. No. This Tamara—the real one, he'd guess—was a survivor and a bare-knuckle brawler who'd sacrifice it all to protect those she loved. "I don't want to cause the team any more headaches than I already have and Essie can't afford to have me lead Jarrod to her location."

"On one condition."

Her eyes went wide, no doubt she'd been expecting another answer. Oh no, he knew better than to run full-tilt at a brick wall and expect it to result in anything other than his head broken open and his brains dripping out. He just needed to keep her off balance. She wouldn't head off right away. No, his girl liked to plan and plot. Snagging Essie and running had probably been one of the few spur-of-the-moment things she'd ever done.

"What condition?"

"Dinner with me tomorrow night." There was no reason why they couldn't get something they both wanted—no matter how she tried to deny it—while at the same time making sure she stayed safe.

She sighed and all but rolled her eyes. "I really don't have time for that."

"No problem. I'm sure the team has plenty of time to hear what kind of trouble you're about to get yourself into by taking off for parts unknown without any backup at all."

Blackmail? Him? Oh, he'd stoop to that and much more. Tamara wasn't the only one willing to go to the mattresses to protect others.

"I'm the last person Taz and Bianca want to help."

It was a nice try. "I suppose that's why they welcomed you into the B-Squad."

"I'm just an office manager, easily replaceable."

That she believed that nonsense was as obvious as her wham-bam-thank-you-ma'am curves. He didn't know who'd worked a number on her head, but someone had scrambled it up but good.

"Uh-huh." Like anyone got upstairs without the full blessing of the B-Squad. "Do you agree or not?"

"Just dinner?"

If there was a God in heaven, no was the answer to that.

"Whatever else is up to you and that little voice inside you telling you to jump my bones like a trampoline, darlin'."

This time she did roll her eyes. "How charming."

"Trust me, my charm isn't what the ladies love most about me." He winked at her, loving the way it put a little pink back in her cheeks. "I'll pick you up after work."

"I'll meet you," she said hurriedly.

More like she'd find a way to ditch him.

"Oh no, darlin'. This is Texas. We have manners. I'll be at your desk to pick you up at five sharp." He tipped an imaginary cowboy hat at her. "Until tomorrow."

As much as he loved watching her walk away—the view was astounding —that's what she expected. With a woman like Tamara, going the expected route was the worst thing possible. It's what made that ice queen facade so easy for her to maintain. What she needed were hurdles and challenges and someone to shake her expectations. He wasn't sure when it had happened

—maybe when he'd offered her that glass of wine at the engagement party and she'd looked at him like he was her own white knight—but somewhere along the line he'd decided to become that someone she needed. Now he just had to show her exactly how good it could be if she let herself melt.

CHAPTER SIX

Tamara

The sun blazed in through Tamara's westward-facing office window. The countdown had begun.

Ten minutes to go before she went to hell...or heaven...or a little bit of both. She didn't fucking know. All she did know was that she was done with the gathering out in the hallway. It had been going on all day. People dropping in for random bits of this or that throughout the day, eyeballing her. Asking her about Isaac. Wondering if she had plans tonight. No doubt gauging whether she was going to go through with the date. As the clock ticked down to five o'clock, most of the B-Squad had taken up observation points outside her office like vultures along the highway eyeing a particularly juicy piece of roadkill. Subtle, they were not.

As she had done all day, she kept her attention focused on her laptop and the billing system software open in front of her. She'd been finishing everything up, leaving lists of what needed to be done in her absence and writing explanations about how to carry on her tasks when she was gone. The numbers and words had all started to blend together an hour ago. She wasn't hiding. She just....she just didn't know what else to do with the anticipation bubbling up inside her with every inch the sun took toward the western horizon.

"Can someone explain to me why every agent I have is glued to the closed-circuit video monitors?" Bianca Sutherland's voice cleared through the quiet buzzing in the hallway. "Are we under attack?"

Not that she welcomed a full-out assault on the B-Squad headquarters, but it would give her an out. One she wanted to take. Didn't she?

"Camacho is in the gym." Keir said, his voice louder than it needed to be.

Was he giving her a heads up in case she wanted to flee or busting her chops? Either was a strong possibility.

"So?" The B-Squad's founder responded.

"He's coming up here next," Vivi said.

Tamara jerked and hit the wrong key, adding an extra set of zeroes to the invoice for the Galligan case as she eavesdropped on the conversation outside her office.

"Again, so?" Bianca asked.

Elisa sighed. "She finally said yes."

"Who?" Taz asked.

"Tamara," Duke replied.

"English please," Bianca ordered.

"After a week of Camacho bird-dogging Tamara, she finally agreed to go out with him." This succinct explanation came from Lash.

"That doesn't explain why you're all out here," Bianca said.

Thank you, Bianca. Now there were three words she hadn't expected to be thinking right about now. Giving up on the pretense of typing, Tamara sat still in her chair, straining to hear the response.

"You really think we'd miss this?" Lexie asked.

A half sigh, half chuckle from Bianca. "Explain to me again what I'm paying you to do."

"Be amazing." This from Vivi—of course.

"The Swan paperwork is on your desk and the research is done on the Snyder case," Marko said.

Bianca stopped in front of the doorway. "We have a flamethrower. Do you want me to clear them out?"

It was tempting. God knew she'd considered setting off the fire alarm. Only the fact that this group was a lot more likely to run toward the flames than away from them had stopped her.

"It's okay," Tamara said. "I can take it."

"I believe that." Bianca strolled inside Tamara's office as if there'd never been anything between them but a simple employer/employee relationship.

They both knew that wasn't the case. Tamara had shown up in Fort Worth with the express purpose of extorting a million dollars out of Taz, telling everyone that she was still married to him. In the process, she'd almost ruined Taz's still new relationship with Bianca. Sure, it had been a desperate move done so she and Essie could go underground and escape Jarrod, but that didn't make it right. It had been easier to justify when she didn't know the team, didn't know Bianca. Now that she'd spent time with the former bad little rich girl made good, the shame of what she'd done twisted her into knots. Bianca had every reason in the world to hate her, but instead of whacking her over the head with a shovel and burying her out in the boonies, she'd given Tamara a job and breathing room to figure out a plan to keep Essie safe.

It was nice while it lasted, but with the bounty hunter showing up at the engagement party she couldn't pretend that Jarrod had forgotten about her and Essie anymore. It was time to take the little stash of money she'd managed to save and get off the grid. If Jarrod couldn't find her, then Essie would have a chance.

It was time to go.

Taking a deep breath, she closed her laptop. "Bianca, I really appreciate everything you've done for me."

Bianca leaned one shoulder against the doorjamb and crossed her arms across her chest. "Why do I hear a 'but'?"

"No 'but'." At least not one she could say. They'd find everything tomorrow, and by that time, she'd be on the road for places unknown. "I know how I came here was wrong. I shouldn't still be here. I'm sorry for that."

"I'm not." Bianca shrugged.

Tamara tried to process what that meant, but couldn't. Of all the people at the B-Squad, Bianca and Taz had more reason to want to see her ass hit the road than anyone else, and she couldn't blame them.

Outside in the hall, the murmurs went silent. The elevator binged its arrival.

There was only one reason for that.

Isaac.

"He's a good guy," Bianca said. "You can trust him."

"How do you know?"

The other woman gave her an understanding smile. "Taz trusts him and that's enough for me."

Tamara tried to imagine what that was like, trusting another human being so much. It was like trying to imagine what sunshine tasted like—a silly fantasy she didn't have time for.

Isaac

The elevator opened up to reveal a human gauntlet. Isaac should have expected it. They'd been giving him shit all week about Tamara. There was no way in hell they were going to miss the chance to bust his balls. It was okay, he had big brass ones.

"You're all a bunch of assholes." He flipped off their grinning faces.

"Camacho." Taz stood in the middle of the scrum, looking every bit like the heavyweight championship boxer he'd been. "Let's chat."

Fuck. Now this he had been hoping to avoid. "Sure, man."

He ducked into Lexie's empty office. The whole place was covered in cats. Inspirational posters on the wall. Figurines. Stuffed animals. Even a life-sized cardboard cutout of a cat in mid-swipe with its claws extended, blood dripping from the edges. The woman had some crazy cat lady shit going on, no doubt about it. He made a mental note not to piss her off. Shit, that could be applied to everyone at the B-Squad.

Taz closed the door behind him and then leaned against it with his arms crossed and a grim look on his face.

Oh, this is going to be a good time.

"You're going out with Tamara?" Taz asked, his eyes narrowed.

Isaac sat down on the corner of Lexie's desk, careful to maintain an unconcerned air even as guilt seeped in. "Was I supposed to ask permission first?"

Okay, Tamara was Taz's ex-wife and the guy code was pretty clear on this, but the rules had never been something Isaac had overly concerned himself with. It was one of the many things that made him a shitty team player.

"No." Taz clenched his jaw tight, obviously as uncomfortable with this chick flick moment as he was. "She's a grown woman who can make her own decisions."

Isaac's shoulders relaxed a few millimeters. He wasn't a part of the B-Squad team. He didn't belong so much as he was B-Squad adjacent, just the way he liked it. But that didn't mean he was good with being persona non grata with Taz and the rest of the team. They'd started to grow on him.

"So what's the problem?"

Taz nailed him with a hard look. "Don't fuck with her."

"What do you mean?"

"You know exactly what I'm saying," Taz said, his voice quiet and deadly serious. "You chased her. Don't think just because she said yes that you caught her."

He picked up one of the small, red wooden cat figurines on Lexie's desk and rolled it in his hand, letting its sharp edges scratch his palm. "Are you warning me or warning me off of her?"

The other man shrugged. "Both."

This really had gone over to the weird touchy-feely side. Was he the bad guy in this situation? Was Tamara? Did it even fucking matter?

"What am I supposed to do with that?"

"Consider it carefully before you do anything stupid." Taz pushed off from the door, his gaze never leaving Isaac.

If they were going to be closed-door dick measuring, he might as well know exactly why. "Is it because she's your ex?"

"It's because she's skating the edge right now," Taz said, his voice harder than a pissed off steer's hooves.

"You don't think I know that?" He knew it. He saw it in the way Tamara was always eyeing the door, the way her body tensed any time someone new walked in a room, the way she'd kept her white-knuckled hands clasped tightly in the cab of his truck after he'd gotten her out of the Corsair Club.

"Yeah, well knowing and giving a shit about it are two different things," Taz shot back.

Heat flared in Isaac's belly. He'd knew every twist, turn and jagged rough patch on that motherfucking edge. With deliberate care, he placed the wood cat on the desk next to Lexie's keyboard and unfurled himself from his sitting position. He had maybe an inch on Taz, but they were well matched and he was done sitting down for a lecture.

"Is that what this is?" He stalked toward the door, infusing each step with snarl and attitude. "Are you giving me the dad talk before I take your darling daughter to prom? That's screwed up."

"Fuck you." Taz took a menacing step forward.

Isaac met him halfway, little jolts of testosterone-fueled adrenaline popping against every nerve. "Likewise, man."

And this was why he didn't do the whole team thing.

Teams had a way of swallowing a man up and leaving nothing behind. He'd been there. Experienced that. He was done sacrificing everything for some supposed greater good that turned out to be just another hill, just another check mark on another man's to-do list that never made a damn bit of difference to the people most affected. Independence wasn't just a word for him. It gave him the freedom to pick and choose his cases, walk away from the bullshit and change what he could for the better. It let him finally wipe some of the red off his ledger—and there was a lot.

He didn't have time for someone else's bullshit.

"Are we done here?" he asked, keeping his stance loose and his gaze steady, ready for whatever was coming next.

"Yeah." Taz pivoted, giving Isaac a clear path to the door. "Good talk."

Isaac didn't look back, didn't hesitate—he walked out the door and into the now deserted hallway. Tamara's office door was open.

She stood next to her window and ran her fingers across the shelf where the black and white photo of her sister Amelia holding her newborn had been the day before. It, along with anything else that marked the office as Tamara's, had disappeared. She faced away from him, but he didn't need to look in those big blue eyes of hers to see the tension stringing her shoulders tight and the anxiousness in the shake of her fingers.

She hadn't left, but she was already gone. He had tonight to convince her that running wasn't the best option. No one knew that better than he did.

Shaking off the last of vestiges of his confrontation with Taz, he dialed up the charm. "Ready for dinner, darlin'?"

CHAPTER SEVEN

Bianca

The elevator opened up to reveal a human gauntlet. Isaac should have expected it. They'd been giving him shit all week about Tamara. There was no way in hell they were going to miss the chance to bust his balls. It was okay, he had big brass ones.

"You're all a bunch of assholes." He flipped off their grinning faces.

"Camacho." Taz stood in the middle of the scrum, looking every bit like the heavyweight championship boxer he'd been. "Let's chat."

Fuck. Now this he had been hoping to avoid. "Sure, man."

He ducked into Lexie's empty office. The whole place was covered in cats. Inspirational posters on the wall. Figurines. Stuffed animals. Even a life-sized cardboard cutout of a cat in mid-swipe with its claws extended, blood dripping from the edges. The woman had some crazy cat lady shit going on, no doubt about it. He made a mental note not to piss her off. Shit, that could be applied to everyone at the B-Squad.

Taz closed the door behind him and then leaned against it with his arms crossed and a grim look on his face.

Oh, this is going to be a good time.

"You're going out with Tamara?" Taz asked, his eyes narrowed.

Isaac sat down on the corner of Lexie's desk, careful to maintain an unconcerned air even as guilt seeped in. "Was I supposed to ask permission first?"

Okay, Tamara was Taz's ex-wife and the guy code was pretty clear on this, but the rules had never been something Isaac had overly concerned himself with. It was one of the many things that made him a shitty team player.

"No." Taz clenched his jaw tight, obviously as uncomfortable with this chick flick moment as he was. "She's a grown woman who can make her own decisions."

Isaac's shoulders relaxed a few millimeters. He wasn't a part of the B-Squad team. He didn't belong so much as he was B-Squad adjacent, just the way he liked it. But that didn't mean he was good with being persona non grata with Taz and the rest of the team. They'd started to grow on him.

"So what's the problem?"

Taz nailed him with a hard look. "Don't fuck with her."

"What do you mean?"

"You know exactly what I'm saying," Taz said, his voice quiet and deadly serious. "You chased her. Don't think just because she said yes that you caught her."

CHAPTER EIGHT

Tamara

Isaac's hand lay on the small of Tamara's back, taking up too much space. It made it hard for her to breathe, hard to think, hard to remember that she had to keep her guard up with this man. He was temptation personified and she had sworn off that months ago. They walked down the block from the Devil's Dip Gym, stopping in front of a familiar jade green door. Satchiko was one of the most hard-to-get-into Japanese restaurants in Fort Worth. The wait list was long and the reviews gushing.

"You like sushi?" she asked as he held the door open and she walked inside the dim interior.

He laughed, the low rumble making her lungs tight. "You say that like I just admitted to licking toads for kicks."

Looking around at the gleaming walnut tables set along a spectacular wall painted in abstract style in bold strokes of gold, blue and green, she couldn't help but let the truth slip out. "It's not what I expected."

He leaned in close, dipping his head down to the shell of her ear and sending a jolt of electricity sizzling across her skin. "You'd figured bad Tex-Mex and cheap beer."

"Maybe." The flush of her cheeks even in the low light had to be enough to tell him just how much of a lie that was.

His hand slid from the small of her back to the curve of her hip, his thumb brushing a lazy circle on the indent of her waist. "When will you realize there's more to me than devastating sex appeal?"

Before she could come up with a smart rejoinder to minimize the uptick in her pulse, the hostess appeared, greeted Isaac by name and ushered them both to an intimate table for two set away from everyone else. He pulled out Tamara's chair and she sat down, trying to remember the protocol for a date. Sure, it had been a while but it should be etched into her bones. God knew she'd been raised to believe it was her only way to secure her future.

Her mother's voice filled her head before she could block it out. *Tits and ass and class—that's how you land a man with money, Tamara Anne. You've got two and can fake the last one if you remember to make the conversation all about him, keep your knees together until he's giving gifts that are weighed in carats and seal your pretty mouth shut ninety-nine percent of the time.*

"If I promise not to poison you, will that make it better or worse?" Isaac asked as he sat down across from her.

The question yanked her out of that dark place in her head where her mother's voice kept up a constant, whispered lecture and she replaced the exhausted worry on her face with a well-practiced smile. "I can see the pros and cons of both options."

She slid her napkin off her plate and smoothed it across her lap, willing her fingers to lose their nervous shake. Why did this man make her nervous? She'd been in the same position with billionaires, superstar athletes, and powerful politicians. None of them made her as aware of every nerve in her body as this man.

He grinned, making her stomach float and her heartbeat speed up. "And to think I left my arsenic at home."

Desperate to regain her equilibrium, she tried to picture his house. Probably lots of leather and wood and sports memorabilia—maybe with remote-controlled mood lighting or an oversized painting of dogs playing poker.

"Now what's that horrified expression for?" he asked, laughing.

"I was picturing what your house looks like."

He shrugged his broad shoulders. "It's a pool house. Lots of flowers and wicker."

"Now that's something I can't even picture." Nope. Isaac was all testosterone and sinewy muscle and sly charm. A dude living in a luau he was not.

"It's temporary," he said, the low tenor of his voice taking on a softer tone. "My mom's had a rough time of it since the accident a year ago."

"What happened?" The question was out before she could stop it, breaking the number-one rule of hooking-a-big-fish dating—keeping things light and fun.

"Drunk driver plowed into my mom and stepfather's car." His gaze dropped to his empty plate for a heartbeat and he clamped his jaw tight before looking back up, a worried anxiety turning his whiskey-colored eyes darker. "My stepfather died. My mom suffered a complex leg fracture, among other things. There was surgery, immobility and then physical therapy. Now she's almost one-hundred percent, which means she's six seconds away from threatening me with a shotgun to go out, find my own place, and hurry up and give her some grandbabies." He finished with a grin that did nothing to eliminate the worry lines carved into his forehead.

"Are you the only child?"

"I'm in the middle of six and the only boy. None of us are married or even looking that way, and it's making her crazier than skillet full of rattlesnakes." This time his smile reached all the way to his eyes.

"Where are you sisters?" Again she broke the dating rules and moved the conversation beyond her date and his many impressive accomplishments.

Isaac didn't seem to care. His whole body relaxed. "They're scattered from here to Alaska. There's Ariella, who flies tourists around in Alaska. Meira and Dalia—forever known as The Twins—run a dude ranch in Montana. Leah just opened up a business selling pot in Colorado. The baby, Shoshana, is about to get her Masters in architecture."

The pride he had in his close-knit family was obvious, and a mix of jealousy and bittersweet regret squeezed her lungs tighter with each breath. It hurt deep in that part of herself she blocked out as much as possible, so she did what she always did. She plastered a pageant-worthy smile on her face and kept the focus off herself.

"I'm trying to picture you growing up with sisters."

"I can do a double French braid in less than three minutes and I've bought more tampons than a thirty-one-year-old man should ever admit to."

Just the mental image of him with his cowboy boots, tight jeans and muscles standing in the middle of the tampon aisle at the grocery store short-wired her brain.

"So what about you?" he asked.

"It was just my mom, Amelia and me." She scrambled for another question to ask about him to return the conversation back to proper lane but her brain wasn't cooperating.

"That's it?" he asked, mock outrage ringing through his words. "No embarrassing stories? Come on. I confessed to buying tampons. If Lash ever found out, I'd never hear the end of it, and eventually, I'd end up with a truck covered in tampons. You know that was a deep dark secret. You owe me the goods."

Shoved mentally off balance by his demand, she didn't think first before letting out the first thing to pop in head. "I stuffed my bra until I finally got boobs."

His focus dipped to her breasts before lifting back up and shaking his head. "Nope. Not good enough."

Secrets? Oh no. She wasn't about to spill those. Embarrassing information? The man already knew she'd tried to blackmail Taz by pretending they were still married. Did it really get any worse than that? She rubbed her temple, the same spot where—

"I got a concussion in a freak baton-twirling accident," she blurted out.

His eyes widened and he settled back in his seat. "Now this I want to hear."

"I was warming up before I was supposed to go on stage at the Miss Garden State Teen competition. I was warming up doing thumb tosses with Tour Jete—"

"Tour whats?" His face was screwed up in question.

It took a second for her brain to make the translation. "So I was tossing the baton up in the air really high and then, while it was in the air, leaping from one foot and making a half turn in the air before landing on the opposite foot."

"That sounds dangerous."

"It can be." Even worse, when her mother was a one thousand on the ten-point pageant mom scale. "I don't know if you've ever been backstage at a pageant, but it's hectic. That night, I thought I'd found a good spot away from the action with enough space to practice, but I wasn't the only one who'd been looking for a little quiet. Another girl found me. I heard a noise, lost my focus for half a second, and the baton came down right on my head. I went down hard."

"So much for winning that crown."

"Oh no. Once I remembered my name again and pounded back some aspirin for my aching head, I grabbed my baton, ignited the flammable ends, did my routine—making sure to always catch the baton in the middle since I was seeing three of them—and won that crown. After that I insisted my mom take me to the ER."

Something that looked like a mix of awe and confusion crossed his face. "You must have fought her tooth and nail to stay in the lineup that night."

"Something like that." More like she'd fought to not go on stage, but she'd lost that battle—just like she'd lost most of the ones she'd waged against her mother until Tamara had finally landed her first sugar daddy. "Actually, the exact opposite. She said she wasn't going to lose out on the investment for the flammable batons and pageant dresses because I was clumsy."

He let out a low whistle. "Wow."

"Yeah." The entire trip to the emergency room had been filled with her mother talking about how this crown was going to be the one to really make a difference in their lives.

"Where is she now?"

"No clue." She hadn't looked back after crossing the GW Bridge into New York. Maybe she should have—maybe she still should—but there were too many times when her mother's voice echoed loud enough in her head to make her think the woman was still beside her, demanding to know when she was going to be bringing money in instead of taking it all out.

The waiter's arrival with a tray loaded down with small glasses and a single bottle stopped that bumpy trip down memory lane.

"Thanks, you always know what I want," Isaac said to the waiter before turning his attention back to Tamara. "Sake?"

She hesitated. It was her last night in Fort Worth. One glass of rice wine wouldn't hurt. Right? "Sure."

The waiter sat the porcelain flask down on the table, a set of two small cups next to it, nodded at Isaac, and then hustled away.

"This is Junmai Ginjo sake." He poured about six ounces of clear liquid into the cup and held it out to her.

"What's that mean?" she asked as she accepted the drink.

"It's been polished—that's when they mill the rice to get rid of the outer layer—to at least sixty percent, and the brewer uses special yeast and fermenting techniques to give it a light, fruity and complex flavor. Smell."

She brought the small cup up to her nose and inhaled, closing her eyes. Icy flowers with a hint of nuts that was both familiar and exotic. "That smells delicious."

"Wait until you taste it." He nudged the ceramic flask toward her. "But first you have to pour for me. It's tradition."

The man was Texas and testosterone personified, and here he was giving her a master class in sake at one of the most exclusive Japanese restaurants in Fort Worth as if he was detailing the value of special teams on the field or how to rebuild a carburetor.

"Isaac Camacho, who are you hiding underneath all that man's man exterior?"

"Darlin', I'm the best of both worlds." He winked at her.

She couldn't help but laugh, an easy camaraderie settling between them. "You are a horrible flirt."

"It's come in handy more times than I can count."

She leaned forward, dying to know more. "Tell me."

And so he did, telling her about backpacking in Peru, an eating tour of Japan, and his stay at an ice hotel in Sweden. Whether it was the sake or the stories, by the time she finished the last small ball of mochito-dusted mochi ice cream, she was as relaxed as she'd been since before her sister had made that fateful call that had led to this quiet moment before she had to go underground again.

"Your face got all serious." Isaac reached across the table and took her hand, circling his thumb over her knuckles. "I swear I didn't really eat the frog raw."

"No, I was just thinking about how I haven't felt this good in a long time." And that it would be the last time for the foreseeable future went unsaid but it sat in the middle of the table between them.

"Being on the run will do that to you."

He wasn't wrong there. "When my sister called, I hadn't talked to her in years. The number showed up as unknown on my phone. How's that for you?"

Hot shame made her skin prickle. She'd been in her latest sugar daddy's Las Vegas hotel suite, staring at the man thirty years older than her as he snored and wondering how in the hell she'd gotten there. As much as she'd fought against her mother, she'd still grown into the exact cold-hearted opportunistic bitch she'd promised herself she'd never be—to the point that she'd barely fought to maintain contact with her sister after Jarrod had weaseled his way into her life.

"You weren't close?" Isaac asked, his voice too carefully neutral.

"That's the thing, despite everything we were close. Growing up, our mom always tried to make us competitors instead of sisters. I don't know why mom did that and I don't care enough at this point to figure it out because it never worked. Amelia was the only one who thought there was more in me than ice."

"So what happened?"

"Jarrod Fane happened. He swept her off her feet, took her back to Idaho, and little by little, he isolated her. In the beginning I tried to keep in touch, but I failed." Unanswered phone calls. Unreturned emails. Texts that went into the void. All of it combined to make a boulder of guilt and regret in the pit of her belly. "For more than ten years there was nothing but silence. By the time she'd finally had enough of Jarrod's bullshit and made a break for it, she was already dying of ovarian cancer and Essie was sixteen. When that call came from Amelia, there wasn't time for anything but making sure Essie was safe."

He squeezed her hand. "She will be."

Emotion clogged her throat, which was ridiculous—a realization that only made the situation worse.

Damn it, Tamara, don't you dare break down in public. You smile. You march forward. You don't ever let them see the cracks.

"Enough of that, my sad story is no way to end such a beautiful meal." She lifted her chin and held up her sake cup. "To no more sad stories."

Instead of raising his glass, he took hers and put it down in the center of the table, his intense gaze burning right through her. "You don't always have to pretend."

She slid her hand from his grasp, missing his heat the moment her fingers cleared his. "And what exactly am I pretending?"

"That you are as cold as you want people to think you are."

"But I am." She'd worked too damned hard to let that safety net of an image go now.

"If that was the case, then you wouldn't be willing to walk away from everything to save the life of a girl you hardly know, even if she is your niece."

"You're not going to change my mind." She balled up her napkin and laid it on her plate, using more care than was necessary to give her an extra few seconds to get rid of the tightness in her throat. "If there's even a single, small percent of a chance that Jarrod knows where I am, it's too much of a risk."

"The B-Squad can protect you," he said, never once looking away from her. "I can protect you."

"Forever? Because that's what it would be. Essie's safe once she turns eighteen and he can't force her to return to Idaho and marry to consolidate his power. But me? I'm on the run for the long haul. Despite the Bible he holds up, Jarrod doesn't forget, forgive, or turn the other cheek. He'll never stop hunting me."

The reality of it slapped her in the face. It was true, even if she'd never said the words out loud before. This was her future. Every bit of resentment, frustration and anger on Jarrod's part would point like a laser beam right at her. He might try to sell his daughter off, if at all possible, but he'd never hurt Essie. He wouldn't give Tamara the same accommodation.

Isaac gave her a considering look. He had more to say, but something over her shoulder caught his attention and his jaw hardened. Glancing over her shoulder, unease creeping up her spine, the only thing she could spot was their waiter, serving a plate of sushi to a couple seated in front of the restaurant's big bay window. In that hyper-aware way waiters had, he looked up and gave Isaac a discrete nod. No doubt their check was on the way. She turned back to the table to find Isaac's attention square on her as he tucked a stack of cash under the corner of his plate.

"You're safe with me." It was a promise tempered with steel—everything she wanted to hear and something she couldn't listen to.

"Oh no, you're trouble of a whole other sort. The kind I like a little too much. And on that note." She pushed her chair back and stood up. "I think it's time to take me back to the garage so I can go home and pack what I need."

He walked beside her toward the door, that large hand of his soft on her lower back, sending little shockwaves of electricity across her skin that teased her with the impossible promise this man offered.

"You're heading out tomorrow morning?" he asked as they walked out into the night, his big body between hers and the street.

"What? No trying to talk me out of it again?" Against her better judgement, she kind of wished he'd try.

"Would it help?" His tone was teasing and he had his trademark grin curling one side of his lips, but he wasn't looking at her. His focus was on the Devil's Dip Gym on the corner, half a block away.

"No. As long as I'm at least one step in front of Jarrod, I'm keeping that lead intact. I really appreciate that yo—"

Before she could finish the thought, Isaac whipped her around and into an alcove in front of a bakery that was closed for the night. The glass door pressed against her back as he eliminated the space between them, dipping his mouth close to hers but not touching. Heart hammering against her ribs, she meant to push against his hard chest but ended up fisting his shirt instead.

"What the hell?" she managed to get out.

"Three guys," he whispered against her overheated skin, his gaze trained on something he could see behind her in the reflection of the bakery's glass window. "They're outside the garage. Don't look. They aren't the usual suspects who hang around outside the gym. I've never seen them before."

Adrenaline raced through her body, putting every nerve ending on high alert. "Jarrod's men."

"Maybe." He pulled her hair back into a ponytail at the base of her neck tight enough to tug her head back so her neck was exposed while her face was turned toward the shadows.

Blood rushed in her ears but couldn't silence the recriminations screaming in her head. She shouldn't have stayed this long. As soon as the bounty hunter had come for her at the engagement party, she should have hit the road. Now it was too late—and she wouldn't be the only one to pay the price, Isaac would too.

"They're coming this way." He stepped closer so that he covered nearly every inch of her. "Take my lead."

"Isaac I—"

His mouth crashed down on hers, blasting away any coherent thought of what she was going to say next. She tightened her grip on his shirt as he gripped her hips, molding her to him even as he kept his heavy-lidded gaze zeroed in on the men reflected in the glass.

CHAPTER NINE

Isaac

Okay, silencing Tamara with a kiss that sent a lightning bolt of lust straight to his balls hadn't been his smartest plan, but circumstance hadn't exactly given him a lot of options.

After spotting the same guy walk past Satchiko's front window three times in the past hour, he couldn't silence the warning buzz making his fingers tingle. As soon as they'd walked out of the restaurant, he'd spotted the same guy in the blue T-shirt lurking across the street, his attention focused on the Devil's Dip Gym. A quick scan of the area revealed a second unknown with a scraggly-ass beard on the opposite corner. The third was slouched down behind the wheel of a sedan parked at the end of the block.

They weren't professionals—too obvious for that—but they weren't lightweights either. Big as fucking tree trunks in some California Redwoods forest, the men watched the gym's entrance and garage door with fanatical attention. He'd seen the type before. Roughly trained, hyped up on one substance or another, and hungry to be the guy to throw the first punch or fire the first bullet. They weren't soldiers. They weren't strategists. They were muscle with specific orders. No doubt, in this case, those orders were to grab, interrogate and dispose of Tamara.

He'd wish them luck but his mama had given him enough home training to know that lying was wrong.

As soon as Red Shirt started strolling their way, Isaac had practically thrown her into the bakery's doorway. He'd moved in and plastered her body to his to block her from view as much as possible. He'd fisted her bright blonde hair so the white-blonde highlights wouldn't glimmer in the streetlight. He'd yanked her head back to keep her face in the shadows. And then he'd kissed her because...well, that was a two-part win that was biting him on the ass, or more correctly, another part of his anatomy. Now was not the time to get a hard-on, but the power shot of adrenaline mixed with lust careening through him had other ideas. Tearing his lips away from hers, but keeping their mouths close enough to make it look like they were kissing from a distance, he took in a deep breath of sanity.

Tamara opened her mouth, but he gave her a gentle squeeze on the curve of her hip and she closed it. The look in her blue eyes told him she didn't like handing her safety over to someone else.

Well, too damn bad darlin', because you're stuck with me.

Primed and ready for action, he continued to block Tamara from view as much as possible while using the bakery's widows to watch the men. Bored Driver and Beard Man maintained their positions. Red Shirt, on the other hand, was strolling his 'roided-up self straight toward them.

Isaac pivoted to completely block the man's view of Tamara. "Don't move," he whispered.

With every step the man took in their direction, the air stilled a little more and the sounds of the city at night came in clearer. A police siren a few blocks away. The laughter of a couple leaving Satchiko. The hum of the traffic on one of the main roads that would eventually spill out onto Interstate 35 West.

Isaac smoothed the visible tension from his body. Even if the guy wasn't a pro, that didn't mean he didn't have good instincts. Fane's outfit was based in Idaho—home to lots of bear, elk and pronghorn hunting. Add to that the fact that The Crest Society took the militia aspect of their twisted little cult seriously, and you had muscle that was just knowledgeable enough to be dangerous.

The man's steps grew nearer. Using the closeness of their bodies to disguise his intent, he glided the back of his palm over the front of Tamara's shirt, noting despite the circumstances the hard pebble of her nipple, and stopped when his fingertips brushed the butt of his Glock. He didn't pull it—not yet, and never unless he had to.

A breeze pulled some of Tamara's hair loose at the same moment Red Shirt passed by them. One long strand whipped her in the face, slicing across her open eyes. Her quick inhale of pain was instinctual and almost silent, but not quite. Red Shirt hesitated. He turned. The man's satisfied exhale was the only warning. It was more than enough.

Keeping his body loose, Isaac looked over his shoulder at Red Shirt, a bored look on his face. "I'm not into being watched man. Take your pervert ass somewhere else."

Red Shirt puffed up his chest. "Let me see the girl first."

"Fuck off." He nudged Tamara another few inches farther back into the alcove's shadows. "I don't share my women."

"I want to see the girl."

"What you want doesn't concern me. Go pound pavement."

He turned back toward Tamara. Her eyes were huge blue dinner plates, but he couldn't do more than give her a reassuring mini-nod before snapping his attention back to Red Shirt's reflection. The big lug stood there for a few seconds, the gears in his walnut-sized brain working hard enough practically make smoke appear.

Definitely not a pro. You didn't hesitate and you didn't telegraph your next move the way Red Shirt was by fisting his meat hook hands.

If he'd been on his own, Isaac would have enjoyed pounding the numbskull into oblivion, but that would leave Tamara exposed, so he went for the move he hated making.

In one fluid move, Isaac withdrew his Glock from the shoulder holster, spun around, extending his gun arm and using his other hand to keep Tamara as far back behind him as possible.

"Here's how this is going to work. Me and my girl are going to make our way to the garage on the corner. You and your buddies are going to stand down."

"Not if that's who I think it is with you." Looked like this broken clock was right at least once a day.

The conversation had ended the moment Isaac pulled the gun. Red Shirt just didn't realize it. As simple as pulling the trigger would be, shooting Red Shirt wasn't the best option. Bored Driver and Beard Man were still at the other end of the block, focused on the Devil's Dip Gym. One loud bang in the night would change that. Fast.

"Hey dipshit," Isaac said, his voice forceful but low.

Red Shirt's gaze flicked from the gun to Isaac's face, exactly as planned.

Isaac adjust his grip on the Glock, brought his arm up and slammed the metal against the man's temple. He went down like a fighter with a glass jaw. There wasn't time to appreciate the victory. He hooked his hands under Red Shirt's armpits and hauled him into the alcove, dropping him at Tamara's feet. He stripped the other man of his Beretta, wallet, and phone, pocketing the last two and handing the gun to Tamara. No one made it a week with B-Squad without at least knowing the basics of gun safety. Like she'd been trained, she kept her finger off the trigger and the muzzle pointed to the ground.

"Follow my lead and we'll get out of here," he promised her.

Her eyes were still wide, but she nodded.

A quick visual sweep showed Bored Driver and Beard Man still at their posts, all of their attention on the gym doors. What he and Tamara needed was a diversion. Lucky for them, the light in the third window from the left on the Devil's Dip Gym's second floor was on.

Keeping his gun pointed at the unconscious thug and the other two goons in his periphery vision, he grabbed his phone and hit the first number on his contact list.

"No after-dinner fun, huh?" Lash asked in greeting.

"Still got a handful of Black Cat fireworks in your desk?"

Marko may be the B-Squad's explosives expert, but he wasn't the only one who loved to see things go boom.

"That counts as one of your weirder questions," Lash said. "Yes."

"I need you to light a couple and toss them out of Tamara's office window on my count." Her window faced the side street. A loud noise coming from that direction would send Bored Driver and Beard Man away from where he and Tamara would be running.

To Lash's credit, the surprised silence only lasted a few seconds. "Do I get to ask why?"

"Later."

The sound of a drawer banging open, some rustling, and then the drawer slamming shut filtered through the phone. "Okay, got 'em." Thirty seconds of dead air. "I'm in position."

"On three, Lash." Isaac scoped out the scene between the bakery alcove and the garage door. "One." The other men didn't even glance this way. Red Shirt must have been a floater. "Two." He gave Tamara one last reassuring look. "Three."

They burst out of the shadows at the same time the night went alive with the snap, crackle, pop of a bazillion fireworks. Beard Man took off at a sprint toward the noise. Bored Driver took his focus off the gym. It was exactly the break they needed. They closed the half a block distance by the time the last firecracker went boom. At the garage's keypad, Isaac punched in his code and pressed his thumb against the scanner. The garage door began rolling up. Bored Driver turned his head, his gaze zeroing in on them. Isaac raised his gun. The other man's lips curled into a cold smile, obviously not so bored any more.

"Tamara, get down and roll under as fast as you can, then hit the red emergency button to close it back down."

She spread her legs shoulder width apart and raised Red Shirt's Beretta. "I'm not leaving you out here alone."

"Darlin', I love your spirit but now is not the time." The garage door inched up.

"I'm not your darling."

It wasn't the time for banter. Shit was about to go down. But before he could open his mouth again, the driver got out.

The guy was easily six-three with a buzz cut and a military-grade automatic rifle in his grip. "Tell me where Essie is and we'll let you go. Jarrod's orders."

Beard Man came tearing around the corner and began approaching from the west. "Tamara, you can't keep a dad away from his baby girl. We'll tell the judge we never laid eyes on you and that we found her on our own."

"Clive, that's only because I'd be dead in a ditch somewhere," she said, the words heavy with disgust. "Now go back and tell Jarrod that he'll never get his hands on Essie again."

Beard Man, a.k.a. Clive, took a step forward, his eyes only on Tamara. "I make it a rule not to lie to Jarrod."

"Yeah, I hear that's an easy way to end up permanently missing," Isaac said, drawing both men's attention off of Tamara as the garage door rolled up. Another few inches and it would be up high enough for her to step back inside without having to dip down and lower her Beretta, then she could hit the emergency release and the door would drop like a lead weight, cutting her off from Fane's men. With her safe behind the secure behind the blast-resistant garage door, Isaac would be free to take them down.

"We're not going anywhere until you talk,"

Sirens sounded a block away and an unmarked black SUV with windows tinted darker than Satan's soul turned the corner. "Oh yes you are."

Even an idiot knew that kind of vehicle meant law enforcement, and not of the local variety.

No doubt figuring adding more guns minus badges to the situation would only escalate things, the team upstairs must have called in Blackfish. Bianca wasn't afraid to throw some B-Squad weight around, but she did it strategically. A bloodbath in front of their headquarters would bring a shitload of bad PR, legal investigations, and even possibly have their Texas state investigations license yanked—none of which was good. So why throw Napalm on the situation when your friendly neighborhood Feds owed you a favor or twelve?

Beard Man hustled toward his car and Fane's other lackey hid his automatic rifle behind his back, scooting toward to the vehicle as Isaac and Tamara holstered their handguns. By the time DEA Agent Clay Blackfish pulled to a stop in the middle of the street between them, Beard Man had his hand on the passenger door and the driver was behind the steering wheel.

"Y'all holding a party in the street without a permit?" the agent asked through the open car window, not bothering to get out of the vehicle.

A second agent sat in the passenger seat, his attention focused on Fane's men. It was impossible to see if the agent had a weapon pointed at the other men but the odds were good.

"Nah, you know me. I'm a homebody," Isaac said.

Blackfish glanced at the other men. "Then y'all better head home."

The driver didn't say anything. He just turned the key in the ignition and started the car's motor purring.

"Don't forget your man down the block," Isaac called out. "We wouldn't want you boys littering up the great state of Texas."

"Littering is definitely a crime," Blackfish agreed. "I'd hate to have a reason to take a look-see at the inside of your vehicle."

Fane's man slowly rolled the car forward, stopped halfway down the block, and pulled over. Beard Man retrieved a groggy but now-conscious Red Shirt and poured him into the car. Then he got in behind him. There wasn't any burning rubber after that, but they weren't taking their time either.

Isaac watched the taillights until they disappeared around a corner. "Thanks Clay. I owe you."

"Your tab is high, but Lash called this one in." Blackfish chewed the end of one of the red coffee stirrer straws he always seemed to have on hand. "I don't know when, but y'all are going to have a huge favor to return someday."

Tamara stiffened beside him. It didn't take a Mensa-level genius to know that she was about as thrilled to owe someone a favor as a struggling surfer was to seeing a passel of sharks headed circling his board.

"We're good for it." Isaac slid his palm across the small of her back, relishing how the tension in her muscles abated even if only a few degrees.

"Better be." Blackfish rolled up the window and drove off down the street.

Isaac turned to Tamara, knowing she wasn't going to want to hear what was about to come next, but the time for keeping the rest of the B-Squad out of this was way past.

She held up her hand and began walking toward her car parked inside the garage. "I'll talk to everyone upstairs first thing in the morning, but tonight I need to go home and get my stuff together."

"You cannot be thinking of going home. Fane's guys could be lurking outside, just waiting for you."

The brake lights on her Camry blinked red and then the trunk popped open. She pocketed the key fob and grabbed another go-bag out of the trunk. "Which is why you're taking me there and staying the night. I have a second car in storage. I'll need a ride in the morning after I say my goodbyes."

The woman was as stubborn as the day was long and as wrong as tits on a boy dog. "You're still determined to leave?"

"I don't have another choice. If Jarrod gets me, he'll do whatever it takes to get Essie's location. Anything. I can't stay here. I need to disappear. It's the only way."

"It doesn't have to be. You have friends upstairs. You don't have to do it alone."

She snorted. "Says the permanent freelancer who won't join the team no matter how many times Taz or Bianca ask?"

Bam. Direct hit. But there wasn't a damn thing the team could do to help him. Some ghosts were impossible to banish.

"Takes one to know one I guess." He swiped the bag from her grasp. "Come on, I'll take you to my place. They won't look for you there."

Tamara didn't even take a single step forward. The bull-headed woman just crossed her arms and got that ready-to-do-battle look in her blue eyes. "There are things at the house that I need."

Something inside him snapped, not at her determination to steer her own ship, but at her refusal to admit even a little that she wasn't one-hundred percent in control.

"What you need to get your head on straight and you can't do that if you're tweaking out on a fading adrenaline rush." He bit out each word. "This isn't a baton twirling concussion. This isn't a desperate attempt to extort money from your ex. This is your niece's life...and yours, damn it, so stop acting like you're the last woman on earth and accept someone's help for once."

The tip of her nose went from pale to raspberry and she gulped. Then he spotted the teary glimmer in her eye. All of the frustration rushing in his veins disappeared in an instant.

Nice going asshole. You're gonna make her cry.

But she didn't. One deep breath and a few inches added to the tilt of her chin, and the ice queen was back—a little thawed but still plenty frosty. Forget giving an inch, the woman wouldn't give a millimeter unless it was pried from her iron grip.

"Wicker and floral prints?" she asked with a snotty sniff.

He won the fight to keep the grin off his face. "There's even a talking fish on the wall."

"You make that thing go off and I'll stab you in your sleep." She strutted past him, stopping at the passenger side of his truck and waited even though they both knew the door was unlocked.

"Just the words every man wants to hear when he's taking a sexy woman home." He strolled over to her side, opened her door, and helped her up into the truck. "Let's go, darlin."

CHAPTER TEN

Tamara

Who would think half a million dollars in twenties could be so heavy? Fifty-five pounds. Tamara knew because she'd weighed it—multiple times —on the digital bathroom scale that had come with her already-furnished rental. When a single woman didn't have television, high-speed Internet, or a library card, she had to make her own entertainment.

She ran her fingers tighter across the duffle bag's nylon straps as she and Isaac sat in his driveway, which was illuminated by the motion-activated security lights that had gone on like a spotlight the moment they'd turned off the road.

"Well, too fucking bad," Isaac said into her cellphone, which was registered to one Margaret Gorman, who'd won the first Miss America pageant in 1921. "She's not coming in right now." He'd swiped it from her hand the second it had buzzed, despite spending the entire drive to his house reading her the riot act for not bringing in the B-Squad from the get-go. "I don't care if you are her boss, Bianca. You're not mine and I'm her ride." After telling Tamara she was a stubborn fool, the last thing she'd expected was him backing her up. "You can pull every last detail out of her tomorrow at eight sharp.Until then, know she's safe." The hard, narrow-eyed look he shot her said exactly how dumb he thought it was that she wasn't talking to them now. One side of his mouth curled upward at something Bianca said on the other end. "No, you smart ass, not all of my dates almost end with a shootout. Then again, I don't normally date women on the run from some crazy-ass cult leader. See you tomorrow."

He hit the end button and powered down her phone before handing it back to her. She slipped it inside the duffle filled with cash, three driver's licenses in the name of former beauty queens, and passports matching each license. In addition, it held one change of clothes, two wigs, and fake IDs with Essie's picture on them. Without a word, Isaac got out and crossed around the front of the truck.

Normally this was when she hurried up and jumped out of the mile-high truck with planet-sized tires before he could help, but she couldn't seem to move. The reality of what had just happened was sinking in like itchy strands of fiberglass. Taking Essie and running from Jarrod had never been a game, but it had never felt as real as it did now.

She was all that was standing between Jarrod and Essie.

The passenger door swung outward, the smell of warm leather, something woodsy, and a whole lotta trouble wafting in off the man holding it open.

"Come on, darlin', you need a decent night's sleep if you're going to face Bianca tomorrow." Isaac held out his hand. "Saying she's pissed you haven't been one-hundred percent truthful with the team—again—is an understatement."

Accepting his help down, even as she refused to hand over the duffle, she ignored the twinge of guilt tweaking her conscience. Bianca's feelings weren't her top priority. Essie was. And that's why she wouldn't be here come morning.

His palm flattened against the small of her back, not pushing, not guiding, just there in a reminder she wasn't alone. It was a weird feeling. It was a nice feeling. It was one she couldn't afford to get used to.

Gritting her teeth together, she marched to the front of the single-story stone building. The driveway had a separate gated entrance from the street from the main drive they'd passed first. This one ended at the back of the pool house, with its artfully weathered wood shutters bracketing the large windows and the iron rooster weathervane perched on top of the roof. She knew money. She'd slept with plenty of men because they'd had it. Isaac—or at least his family—had it. All the instincts she'd spent a lifetime honing buzzed to life.

"You have to look at them like they're another diamond to add to your tiara. It's not about what you want, Tamara. It's about protecting yourself for later. Do you really think I'd be living in this dump if I'd used what I had when I had it? No. If I hadn't met your father, I'd still be in New York without a care in the world." Her mother looked around the crowded two bedroom apartment, picking up one of Amelia's library books off the thrift-store couch and tossing it aside like trash. "Instead, here I am with you two."

She closed her eyes and shut out her mother's voice. She'd been twelve when her mother had passed along that little gem of advice to mark the occasion of Tamara's first period.

The duffle's nylon handle dug into her hand, each of the fifty-five pounds wearing on her grip. It didn't hurt though. It was a good kind of pain, the kind that reminded her she didn't need a rich man's money to survive. She had her own and could make it last for a long time where she was planning to go.

"You know I can see the gears turning in that pretty head of yours, right?" Isaac asked as he unlocked the front door and pushed it inward. "But before you put your plan into action, how about a drink?"

"I think I've had enough." Between the sake and the adrenaline rush, she was feeling high enough already.

Isaac followed her inside, shutting the door behind them and arming the alarm system. "When you've just stared down the barrel of an automatic rifle and managed not to get shot or pee your pants, you should have a drink."

She chuckled despite herself. "I guess you'll be having water only?"

"Hell, I only peed a little." He grinned. "I'm getting a beer too." He strolled over to the fridge.

She sat the duffle down on the coffee table and looked around the pool house. He hadn't been lying about the floral or the wicker...or the talking fish on the wall. What he'd failed to mention was the custom-designed mosaic tile floor or the original David Hockney painting that had sold for more than five million at a Sotheby's auction. She'd known because her much-older boyfriend at the time had been hoping to get it himself.

She walked around the floral couch and the dark brown wicker end tables, her heels clicking on the hardwood floor, until she stood in front of the large painting.

Isaac stopped beside her and handed her a beer bottle cold enough to give her a shiver. At least that's what she told herself had caused the reaction rather than being so close to a man who made it damn hard to remember why she was in his house in the first place. She sipped the beer, the crisp taste of the lager doing nothing to distract her from him. Every sense seemed heightened, every nerve primed. Post-adrenaline sex rush, the girls at the office called it.

Neither said a word as they drank in silence and stared at the painting of felled trees done in vivid greens and delicate browns with purple and red wildflowers dotting the bucolic scene. She still she could feel him—the heat of his body, the ghost of his palm against her back, the tangible need vibrating between them.

"Thinking about taking it when you sneak out at dawn?" he asked, curling an arm around her back and letting his fingertips rest on the swell of her hip. "Please do, the damned thing is uglier than a rodeo clown after last call."

The play of his fingers scrambled her brains and sent a rush of heat straight to her core. "What makes you think I'm leaving?"

The handsome bastard had the audacity to laugh. "Like I said darlin', I can see the gears turning."

"So you're a mind reader?" She pivoted on the ball of her foot as she said it, knowing the move was a mistake but unable to stop it.

His fingers slid from her hip, following the waistband of her skirt to the small of her back as she turned and burning a line of fire through her clothes that made it hard for her to breathe, to think. Feeling? Oh that came far too easy when she was with him.

"Nope." He tightened his grip just enough to bring her a few inches closer, enough that she couldn't miss the way his eyes had darkened with desire. "Just someone who recognizes stupid ideas because he's had so many of his own."

Anger sparked. "Leaving isn't stupid." She pressed a hand against his rock-hard chest but made no progress in putting any more air between them.

"Course it is," he said, lazy confidence thick in his voice. "Jarrod has proven he's not giving up. Where are you going to go in the United States that he won't eventually track you down?"

"Who said I'm staying stateside?"

One eyebrow shot up. "Oh, so you want to be a million miles away for when he finally gets a bead on his missing daughter's location. That's an even worse plan."

"He won't find her." She said it like she believed it. She had to. It was the only card she had left to play.

"Yeah, that's what you thought about him finding you."

The words were quiet, said with a soft kindness, but they left her scorched. "So what do you suggest, I give up?"

"Hell no." He shook his head. "What I'm saying is that you use the resources at your disposal to neutralize him."

Jeez, if only she'd thought of that. Too bad she didn't have resources beyond a bag of cash and the ability to take Essie's location to her grave. "Are you volunteering to put a bullet in Jarrod's brain?"

He started, releasing his hold and taking a step back, his moves stiff. "I don't kill people unless there's no other choice."

"Me either, which is too bad because that's what it's going to take to make him stop. That's why Essie's best option is for me to go so far underground that I don't even make a lump in the dirt." Her voice had risen with each word until she was practically yelling in the pool house's quiet interior, drowning out the soft hum of the air conditioner.

Breathing hard, she stared at Isaac, daring him to tell her she was wrong.

Instead, he laughed. Hard. "A lump in the dirt?" He took a long swig of beer. "That makes no fucking sense."

"Well, not all of us are as good with bullshit cowboy metaphors as you are."

He stepped closer, took her beer so he held both of them in his sure grasp and then sat them down on the end table. "You need to talk to Bianca and the team tomorrow. Together we can come up with a plan."

This again. Didn't he understand? He should. He was the one Taz had turned to for a background check on her after she'd shown up in Fort Worth and tried to extort a million dollars out of him by swearing up, down and sideways that they were still married. Isaac knew how to do his job. There was no way the man hadn't found every skeleton in her walk-in closet —and there were a lot of them, too many. There were people out there who deserved the B-Squad's help to right a wrong, and she wasn't one of them.

"They have no reason to help me."

"They have every reason, but if you can't get that through your thick skull then do it for Essie. Doesn't she at least deserve to have people fight for her?"

Denial. Desperation. Dread. They battled it out inside of her and the only thing she could do to manage it was bring in the cold, the icy indifference that numbed everything. But it wouldn't come. Around Isaac, it so rarely did. So instead she met his fire with some of her own. Worst of all, he was right and she knew it. Belize wasn't going to happen, not until she knew Essie was safe. She couldn't risk being that far away. She needed the B-Squad. Not that this realization made her feel any better. Hell no. It just pissed her off more.

Hands planted on her hips, she glared up at him. "You think you have all the answers don't you?"

"Not even close," he said, his voice as soft as hers had been hard. "But I do know this: running away from bad shit never makes it go away, hiding doesn't either."

She sank down and half-sat, half-leaned against the back of the couch. "I don't know what else to do."

He hooked a finger under her chin and tilted it upward so she couldn't avoid looking him in the eye. "Let me help you."

Something in her stomach fluttered. Attraction? Hope? Belief? She didn't know. What she did know is that this wasn't how her life went. With only a few exceptions like Amelia and Albert, people didn't help. They were impediments to be avoided and hazards to be guarded against. Anyone who offered help had to have something in it for them. But Isaac didn't—at least nothing she could see—and it confused her as much as it thrilled and scared her.

"You're not going to give up on that are you?" she asked with a sigh.

"I'm always glad to help." His grin was as quick and easy as it was devastating to her panties. "What can I say? I'm a real dick that way."

The angry tension stringing her tight evaporated, her answering chuckle genuine. But with every second she and Isaac stayed like that, she became more aware of a different type of tension growing between them.

Anticipation made the air heavy, like the sky before the first crack of thunder during a summer storm. His gaze dropped down to her lips, to her cleavage, to the hard tips of her nipples pressing against her thin shirt, then to the apex of her thighs where desire had turned her core slick. She'd been naked before and never felt so exposed. It was totally freeing. What was left for her to hide behind her ice walls if he already knew what she was? She was a bitch. She was an opportunist. She was willing to do whatever it took to get what she needed. He wanted her anyway and God knew she wanted him. Why couldn't they both come out ahead, at least for tonight?

She rose to her feet, lining her body up with his and closing the gap between them. "What if I need help in a different way?"

"Darlin', I'm a full-service kind of helper." His hand dropped to her left hip, sending a jolt of awareness straight to her clit. "You tell me what ache is building and I'll relieve it." His other hand fell to her right hip and he pulled her close. "Tell me where it itches and I'll scratch it." His cock, hard and thick, pressed against her, letting lose a wave of desire that threatened to overwhelm her. "Show me where it hurts and I'll kiss it better."

"You make a lot of promises," she managed to get out, trying to string out the inevitable for just a few moments longer, because once she gave in there was no going back.

"And I'll deliver on every single one." He dipped his head lower, letting his lips brush across hers. "You can count on it."

CHAPTER ELEVEN

Isaac

He loved women. Loved their curves, their softness, their tempting sense of possibility. Tamara had all of that, but that wasn't what shot a bolt of lightning straight to his cock. No. It was her edges, her hardness, her tantalizing cryptic promise. It was that she didn't surrender in his arms so much as throw down a gauntlet and—with a teasing wink—ask him what he was going to do about it. There was no way in heaven or hell he wouldn't pick it up.

The moment he brought his mouth down to her half-parted, full lips, they both knew what it was—a challenge accepted. He swept his tongue inside her hot mouth, deepening the kiss as he pulled her against his hard dick. Fuck, he wanted her. He had from the moment he'd clapped eyes on her after compiling her extensive background file. Now he was going to have her.

She undulated against him, her hips rocking against him with an urgency that had his eyes crossing. The sweet friction almost made up for the lack of skin-to-skin contact, but he'd never been a man for almost. He wanted her wet, naked, and moaning underneath him, on top of him, and any other way he could get her. The options were endless.

He dragged his lips from her luscious mouth to her jaw. "Wall," he said against her skin. "Couch." He kissed his way to the spot where her ear met her throat. "Kitchen counter." He sucked her earlobe into his mouth, grazing his teeth across her flesh. "Dining room table." He made his way down the slim column of her throat, over her fluttering pulse point, to the base. "Bed."

"I can only pick one?"

He slipped a button on her shirt free. "Darlin', that's the order of events, not a list of either-or."

"You really think you're up for that?" she teased, rubbing up against the proof of exactly how ready he was.

"Are you?" He made quick work of her remaining buttons but didn't spread her shirt wide. The strip of visible creamy flesh mesmerized him. "I think you are." God knew he could feel her heat against him. "I think you're wet and ready for me already."

She arched her back, making the material of her shirt slip a few inches back and revealing more of her tempting flesh. "Only one way to find out."

"One way?" He traced a single finger across the upper swells of her tits, avoiding the hard points of her nipples pressing against the thin material of her bra even though it almost killed him to avoid the sensitive peaks. "That shows a serious lack of creativity."

She took half a step back, the look in her eyes promising he'd like whatever came next, so he let her go. Never looking away from him, she reached down to the skirt covering her from her firm thighs down to her knees and slowly inched it up. His cock twitched with every bit of leg exposed. By the time she'd scrunched the material high enough so she could spread her legs hip-width apart, he was listing world capitals in his head to keep from grabbing her and fucking her over the back of the couch. The sheer black of her panties showed as much as it covered. Much like the woman herself, they gave away only enough to drive him right up to the edge of crazy and make jumping over seem like the best idea ever.

Looking up at him with a desire-hooded gaze and a smile as sinful as cake and ice cream for breakfast, she curled her lips into a knowing smile. "Give me your hand."

Like he was going to say no. He held it out, palm up. She snagged her bottom lip between her teeth and took his hand in her much smaller one. His whole body hummed with expectation as she pulled his hand between her spread thighs and pressed it to her damp panties.

"You tell me," she said, lust a low thread stringing her words together. "Am I wet enough for you?"

If he could have formed words at the moment he would have, but that wasn't going to happen. A switch had flipped and the only thing that mattered in the world was making the woman in front of him come.

"That's enough teasing." He dropped to his knees, whipping her panties down with him before clamping his hands on her hips. He held her place, his fingertips pressing into her full ass and his thumbs as close to the apex of her thighs as he could get.

"Who said I was teasing?" she asked, a sexy little catch in her voice. "You asked a question and I answered...creatively."

Smart ass. "Can you stay still, or do I have to hold you in place?"

"Depends." She looked down at him and wove her fingers through his hair, tugging the strands harder than she needed to. "Are you any good?"

"Darlin, I'm gonna rock your world so hard you just might pull out half of my hair in the process." And it would be worth it to hear her scream in ecstasy.

She gulped and that bitchy, always-in-control facade of hers wavered. "You'd better hold onto me then."

He did, pushing her back just enough that her ass was against the back of the couch. Every taut line in her body told him she expected him to just dive in. Instead, he ran his tongue up the inside of her smooth thigh, skipped over the most inviting spot at the top, and kissed his way over the top of her bare mound. Her body went still and tense as he got closer to the tip of her clit peeking out through her glistening lips. His hands still grasping her hips, he looked up at her as he skipped over that bundle of nerves and tasted his way down the inside of her other thigh.

She let out a frustrated sigh and her head dropped back. "You're not nice."

"Are you just figuring that out?" he asked, forcing a lightness into his tone that was at odds with near blinding desperation to taste her.

"Isaac, please." She pushed against his hold on her hips, drawing his attention exactly where they both wanted it to be.

"What do you want?" He tightened his grip on her hips and drove her back against the couch, refusing to touch her anywhere else even though her perfect, pink pussy was at mouth level and he was dying to taste her.

"You know," she pleaded.

"Don't turn shy on me now." He leaned in and blew a breath across her. "Tell me."

"I want your tongue on me."

He loosened his hold on her hips and glided his palms to her thighs, spreading his fingers wide so his thumbs rested on her inner thighs only inches below her core. "Where?"

"My pussy." It was an appeal, a surrender, a dare—she would never present only one answer, not even in a moment like this, not even with two simple words.

"How do you want it, darlin'?" He rubbed soft circles with the pads of his thumbs that moved higher with each rotation. "Slow? Fast? Hard? Gentle? Fingers? Sucking? Licking? Fucking you with my tongue?"

She bucked against his hold and thrust her hips forward so her sweet, glistening center was only inches from his mouth. "Yes."

"Good. That's my favorite."

The first lap was slow. He took his time to taste her, to feel her thighs shake under his palms, to hear her unmuffled moan of pleasure. All of it made his cock harder than he thought possible, but he wanted—needed—more. He wet a finger in his mouth then slid it home inside of her before adding a second and twisting them around so he could flick them against her G-spot. She threw her head back, grinding her core against the flat of his palm as he enjoyed the taste of her clinging to his lips.

"Damn." He muttered the curse into her wet center, then glided his tongue along her inner lips and circled her clit, licking and sucking her without mercy as she rotated her hips and pushed against him.

Lost in her wet softness, he took her with his mouth, slow then fast, hard and then soft. He added and withdrew fingers in response to the way she trembled and mewled her pleasure, wanting to take her higher with each stroke and lick.

"Yes," she cried out, her voice strangled with desire.

His fingers slid in and out, stretched her open while his tongue continued its dance. Millimeter by millimeter, his flat tongue slid up her wet lips. He stopped at her clit, sucked the warm nub into his mouth.

She yanked on his hair and rocked against his tongue as her core tightened around his fingers. Close. She was almost there. All he needed to do was give her a little push and she'd explode over the edge. He curled his fingers so he could reach the tight bundle of nerves just inside her entrance as he plunged them inside her and sucked hard on her hard clit. Her entire body tightened as she let out a hoarse "yes" and came against his mouth, sweet and hard and free.

Rolling back onto his heels, he wiped a hand across his mouth before standing. Her blue eyes were half-hooded, her cheeks pink and her breathing labored as she watched him. Instead of firing off a smart remark, she reached behind her back and unclasped her bra, slid the straps down her arms and dropped the scrap of material to the floor beside her discarded panties.

"Check off the couch." Her arm shot out and she shoved him back until his ass hit the drywall. "Now for the wall."

Tamara

Her legs might still be made of Jell-O after that orgasm, but there was no way Tamara was waiting any longer for Isaac's cock. She was many things, but patient when it came to getting what she wanted wasn't one of them, especially not with blind lust threatening to burn her from the inside out.

She latched onto his leather belt and slipped it free of the buckle. "Take off your boots."

"You're still wearing your shoes," he said, his voice husky.

Raising herself to her full height in the four-inch heels—which still brought her almost half a foot shy of Isaac's six feet four—she pressed her naked body to him and relished how her body lined up almost perfectly with his thanks to her stilettos. The tightening in his jaw and flare of desire in his dark brown eyes proved she wasn't the only one to appreciate the added height.

"Are you asking me to take them off?" She slid her hands between their bodies and popped the button of his jeans open.

"Fuck no."

"Good." She yanked his zipper down and slipped her hand inside the opening of his boxers, wrapping her fingers around the hard steel of his cock. "Take them off. Take it all off."

Hating to let him go, she did and took a step back to watch the show. Grinning, no doubt because he knew damn well she wanted to watch, he pulled off his boots slowly and followed up by leisurely getting rid of his jeans, shirt, and boxers, exposing one small square of light brown skin at a time. By the time he was standing before her without a stitch on, she'd forgotten how to breathe.

Her imaginings of a bare-naked Isaac had been hot. The real thing was scorching. Broad shoulders. Thick thighs. Defined, sinewy arms. A dusting of dark, curly hair across hard pecs, drifting down over rippling abs to end at the base of an impressive cock, the swollen tip already wet with pre-come.

"Damn." And that was the honest truth.

He winked, the cocky bastard. "The feeling's mutual, darlin'."

She should make him wait, but she couldn't keep her hands off him any longer. His chest hair sprung back against her fingers, tickling her palms as she glided them down his chest. He stood still underneath her touch—silent for once—but there was no missing the hammer of his heart under her hand. She dipped her head and lapped at the hard point of his nipple.

"I suppose you're going to draw this out."

"Turnabout is fair play." She trailed her fingers over the flexing muscles of his abdomen and encircled his dick, holding him tight.

He exhaled a sharp breath and the back of his head hit the wall with a thunk. "You're mean."

Sinking down to her knees before him, she kept her face tilted upward so she could watch his face. "And you love it."

Whatever he was about to say was swallowed by a strangled groan the second she swirled her tongue over the head of his cock. She kept one hand at the base and took him in as deep as she could before retreating and repeating the process, engulfing him a little bit more each time. His thigh was tree-trunk hard underneath her left hand. Even as she took him in, she had to touch, to explore, to know him. Her fingers wandered, caressing his leg, reaching up over his lean hip, tracing across his muscular abs.

Blowjobs weren't part of her normal routine, but when had anything with Isaac been even remotely close to normal? The closest it got was the fact that he obviously had more money in his bank account than he let on with his worn-in jeans and his mid-mileage truck. And for the first time in longer than she could remember, it didn't matter. That wasn't why she was here sucking him. It was because she wanted to, pure and simple. She wanted to make him feel good, to hear him lose control, to give him one heart-stopping moment of total bliss—and not because she was trying to pay him back for helping her, but because she couldn't imagine anything better.

He groaned. "God you look good like that."

She let his cock go with a quiet pop but kept her right hand stroking the hard length of him. "I always look good."

"I know where you'd look even better."

Something flashed in his eyes that made her shiver in the best of all possible ways. Then, lightning fast, he hooked his hands under her arms and hauled her up to a standing position. On her next breath she was in the air before being tossed over his shoulder like a bag of potatoes. The position gave her an unprecedented look at his very perfect ass, which she smacked.

"What are you doing?" she asked, smiling despite all the blood rushing to her head.

"Taking you somewhere horizontal." His sure stride bypassed the kitchen.

"What about the counters?" She caught a glimpse of a long, wooden table before he turned down a hallway lit only by the moonlight coming in through a large skylight. "Or the dining room table?"

"Next time."

"Who said there'd be a next time?"

He turned into a moonlit room. "Darlin', get back to me in a few hours and let me know if you haven't figured out the answer to that one."

Her core clenched. One orgasm had made her greedy for more. "You're awfully confident."

"And you love it."

He wrapped his hands around her waist and did some kind of shoulder pop thing and she went sailing through the air, landing with a soft thump in the middle of a giant mattress. It was exactly where she wanted to be.

Isaac

Damn, she looked good spread out on his bed. Isaac's dick was as hard as a steel-coated two-by-four, but he had to take a moment to appreciate the way the moon turned her long, blond hair silver, how her full tits bounced when she'd landed, and the way her legs went on and on and on as she spread them wide. One look at the glistening softness of her pink pussy and observation time was over. He stormed over to the bedside table and yanked the drawer open, grabbed a condom, and laid it on the top of the table where it was in easy reach.

Tamara had rolled onto her side, her fingers lazily playing with the tips of her nipples, pinching and stroking them. She was close to the edge of the bed, her mouth already open, her tongue wetting her lips. The invitation in her eyes snapped what little bit of control he still had.

He was on his knees, the bed sinking beneath him and his dick sliding into her hot mouth before he had time to process the move. The gentle swipe of her tongue around him as she sucked napalmed what was left of his brain. She took him deep and swallowed. Pleasure rocketed through his body, making him almost ache with it. Then she did what she always did—she surprised him. The little tease skimmed one hand down over the full curve of her tits, down the flat plane of her stomach and to the juncture of her spread legs. He didn't know where to look. Her fingers playing with her swollen clit or his cock disappearing between her slick lips? He'd fucking sell his soul to be able to watch both at the same time.

That was it. Tamara was going to kill him. He'd never looked so forward to dying.

"Does that feel good, darlin'? You want to be all filled up?"

She moaned around his dick and his balls vibrated with mind-melting pleasure, but it wasn't enough. It couldn't be unless she was right there with him, skating along the edge.

"Let me help." He reached over and put his fingers on top of hers and she stilled. "No. Show me. Let me feel how you make yourself come."

Another lusty moan around his cock as she sucked and stroked him with her mouth, then she swirled her fingers around her clit using the fingertips of two fingers with a slow, light touch. Tangling his fingers in her silky hair, he held her head still so he could match the stroke of his cock into her mouth with her leisurely pace circling her sensitive nub. Watching her, fucking her mouth, letting his fingers slide down so that he could dip inside her opening. She arched against his hand, rocking against his fingers.

"Is this how you touched yourself when you thought about me?"

She pulled away from his hold on her head and let him slip from her mouth. "What makes you think I've pictured you while masturbating?"

Feisty. Her attitude turned him on just as much as her traffic-stopping curves. "Because I sure as hell have pictured you."

"Tell me." Breathy. Needy. Heat so hot she'd burn with a blue flame.

This was the real Tamara—not the ice queen she showed the world. She was a sight to behold and he counted himself damn lucky to be getting an up-close-and-personal view—and if he didn't get even closer soon he was going to lose it. He withdrew his fingers and tasted her sweetness before stepping down off the bed and reaching for the condom on the bedside table.

"You want to hear about all the ways I've fucked you in my mind?" He tore open the foil wrapper.

She licked her lips as she watched him roll the condom on. "Yes."

He grabbed her legs at the ankles and spun her around on the bed, spreading her legs as he ran his hands up the outside of her calves, knees and finally up to her thighs so that he stood between them. "No."

"No?"

"I'd rather show you."

"Lucky me."

She hooked her ankles together at the small of his back. The move pulled him closer to where he wanted to be and let him slide his palms up and around so he cupped her ass and lifted her hips higher. He lined up his straining cock with her entrance.

"Which of us is the lucky one is up for debate, but not at this moment because I can't wait any longer for this."

He slid home in one long, excruciatingly amazing stroke until he was buried balls-deep in her clinging warmth. Better than he'd imagined? Hell, he hadn't even come close. Sensation bombarded him as he withdrew and plunged forward, his whole body was buzzing and alive. The whole world disappeared. There was only them.

Her body responded to his rhythm, increasing the pace and arching her hips upward to take more of him, let him hit that bundle of nerves just inside her entrance. As soon as he did, she squeezed around his dick like a hot fist.

"Isaac," she moaned as she rotated her hips and angled her body so that only her shoulders touched the mattress.

"How can I make it better, darlin'?" He'd do it. Whatever it took.

"Fast. Hard. Now."

Her wish was his command. She met each of his forceful thrusts, their bodies urging each other toward that sweet spot where pleasure bordered on blissful agony. A strangled moan escaped as her orgasm exploded and she clamped down on him, holding his cock tight.

He drove into her, his balls slapping against her bare flesh. The tempo increased to a frantic rhythm, ecstasy laying just beyond her reach. The pressure swelled until it consumed him. In an instant, the world shattered as he plunged inside of her one last time, coming with her name on his lips.

Their breathing was ragged and satisfied. Every bone in his body weighed a thousand pounds. Letting go of her wasn't something he wanted to do, but logistics was a bitch that way.

"I'll be right back." He got rid of the condom in the world's fastest trip to the bathroom.

Before he could dive under the covers and pull her close though, she had both feet on the ground and a pinched look on her face. He knew that look. It was the oh-shit-what-have-I-done look. God knew he'd worn it often enough after some of his crazier nights. But this wasn't one of those nights.

So much for a warm, fuzzy, post-coital feeling. "Having second thoughts?"

Her chin went up ten degrees. "No."

His gut gave a twinge. "Then what?"

"I should shower." She smoothed her hair. "I'm all sweaty and my hair's a mess."

Oh hell no. He didn't know who in the world had fucked with her enough that she confused a sexy, just-been-fucked afterglow with being dirty, but he would very much like to shove his fist down the asshole's throat.

"Darlin', I like you just the way you are."

She giggled. "Are you stealing lines from Bridget Jones's Diary?"

"I do have five sisters." Taking advantage of her moment of distraction, he tugged her down to his side, letting go of a breath he didn't realize he was holding when she rolled onto her side and laid her head in the pocket of his shoulder. "I've watched every rom com there is."

"Oh, and you even know the lingo."

He could feel her smile against his skin. It felt good. Really good.

"Don't start with me, Tamara Post."

"Does that mean you're finished already?" she teased.

"Not even close." He wrapped an arm loosely around her waist. "Sleep while you can. I'll be waking you up in the best of ways in an hour."

"Promises. Promises," she half sighed, half mumbled.

He turned his head and brushed a kiss across her forehead. "You know I always keep them."

Tamara said something, but her words were too faint to understand. Her deep, steady breathing told him everything he needed to know. Relaxing back into the pillow, his own eyes drooping, he picked up the tablet on the bedside table to triple-check that all of the security systems were engaged. He'd promised Tamara she'd be safe with him. He wasn't about to break that pledge. One glance at the proprietary app he'd designed confirmed that anything bigger than a gnat would trip the alarms. That plus the beautiful, complicated woman asleep in his arms was all it took to knock him out for the night, and with any luck, it would banish the recurring nightmare he'd brought back with him from Afghanistan.

CHAPTER TWELVE

Tamara

The sun was still a soft pink line on the horizon when Tamara started carefully scooting out from underneath Isaac's arm. It was a delicate procedure. Waking him up wasn't a good idea. There were things in the duffle that needed her—and only her—attention. The B-Squad was plan A, but if that fell through she needed to make sure plans B and C were already in motion, and that meant solo access to what was in the duffle. Her lungs tight from holding her breath, she'd made it from being flush against his naked body to almost the edge of the bed that seemed as big as Texas when his strong fingers curled around her waist and tugged her back against his hard form.

"Going somewhere?" Isaac asked, nuzzling the back of her neck.

The husky, sleep-roughened gravel in his voice set off a flurry of kamikaze butterflies in her stomach. "I wasn't sneaking out."

"Really?" He nibbled his way down the column of her throat.

It was really hard to come up with a plausible cover story when he did that. It made her brain foggy and the rest of her soft and wet. "Okay, I was sneaking out of bed, but that's it. Most human beings do have to pee after they wake up."

"And you just naturally wake up at..." He let go of her and reached past her to swipe his phone of the bedside table. He squinted at the screen. "God, that can't be right. Do they actually make a time this early? That's wrong."

He put the phone back and brought her in tight against him again, close enough that there was no doubt that not all of him was still asleep. She shouldn't stretch so her bare ass rubbed against his fast-stiffening cock. It was wrong...he had other things to do...but it felt so good.

He groaned and cupped her breast, rolling her nipple between his fingers.

"Not a morning person?" she asked, as if she wasn't doing her best to wake all of him up.

"Darlin'..." He took a soft nip of her shoulder. "I'm more of a wee hours of the morning person."

The temptation to keep pushing, to just lay in bed and tease him until he couldn't take it anymore was so strong it almost made her forget everything that was at stake. Almost. Her mother may not have taught her the best lessons in life, but she'd given her an up-close and personal class on the most important one: Don't ever expect anyone to come to the rescue. Fate favored the hustler.

"Go back to sleep." She slipped his hold and scooted across the bed in the next breath. "We're not due at headquarters for another couple of hours. I'll just take care of a few things."

"Like what?"

Plane reservations. Buying a new piece of shit car to cross the border in. Hair dye. Working up some fake personas online to make her fake identities more realistic. "Shower. Get ready. Girl stuff."

He curled his body in one smooth motion so he was sitting up in bed staring at her, the sheets tangling in his lap and the morning sun touching the hard planes of his chest. "So why do you have the duffle?"

Damn, the man was persistent. "It's got a change of clothes."

She grabbed the duffle off the top of his dresser, ignoring the tug of the extra twenty pounds on one side, and hustled toward the bathroom and the door she could lock shut between them.

"Not to mention half a million dollars and a bunch of fake IDs."

She jerked to a stop and whirled around to face him. The smug satisfied look on his face just torqued up her annoyance. "You went through my bag?"

"Three in the morning and I are old friends."

"What, is that when you think about how awesome you are?" she put just enough disgust in her voice to make each word transform into a slap across his square jaw.

His eyes darkened to almost ebony, but he wasn't looking at her. He was gazing at something in the distance with a weary, mile-long stare that said too much without saying anything at all. Whatever haunted Isaac at 3 in the morning, it was eating away at him one chunk at a time—and she'd rubbed his face in it because he'd done the thing he was trained to do and left no stone unturned and no duffle unopened when it came to keeping her safe.

Tamara Post, you are a royal bitch.

Admitting this wouldn't help. No one knew better than she did that some wounds were best left unexplored. So instead of apologizing, she did what she always hoped others would do when her facade cracked. She pretended it hadn't happened.

"What, am I a prisoner?" Her tone didn't have the bitter heat the question required. "Do you want to watch me shower next?"

His attention snapped back to her and, in a heartbeat, the torment was gone from his eyes. "No, and yes, but for totally different reasons than you're insinuating." He drew out the Texas drawl, no doubt because he knew exactly what it did to her equilibrium.

Maybe it was nerves. Maybe it was because of the way he looked at her. Maybe it was because it was hard to stay annoyed with a man who hid his hurt behind enough charm to catch all the girls in the state. Whatever it was, the giggles escaped before she had a chance to squash them. For his part, Isaac put his hands behind his head and leaned back against the pillows, a sexy grin playing at the corners of his mouth.

Her shoulders relaxed as the tension ebbed from the room. "Look, I'm not doing an Irish goodbye, but I do need to get some things in place just in case."

"Always a plan B, huh?"

"C, D, and E too." And wasn't that the truth.

"And you don't care to enlighten me as to what those plans are?"

"Essie is safer if fewer people know."

"Keeping you safe would be a lot easier if you trusted me."

"It's not you."

"You don't trust anyone."

"I trust my gut." And it was telling her to get her ass in the bathroom and start setting everything in motion, because the more time she spent with Isaac, the softer her edges got. She needed those sharp lines. Fuck the world before it fucked you first. The mantra was tattooed on her soul.

He narrowed his eyes, way more observant than a person would assume considering the pretty packaging. "What's your gut saying?"

The truth slipped out before she could stop it. "That you're too tempting by half."

He laughed, the big booming sound echoing in the room. "Go take your shower. I'll get breakfast started."

She strolled into the attached bathroom. "Black coffee is good enough for me."

"I don't think so." He shook his head. "My mom would skin me alive for having guests over and not feeding them properly."

"You really know how to cook?" she asked as she laid the duffel on the floor in the bathroom.

"Trust me," he said, his voice dropping a few octaves to the low rumble that made her thighs clench. "I could teach you a thing or two."

That her hand only trembled the slightest bit as she closed the bathroom door would have to go down as a top ten moment of triumph. The man was sex personified, and after last night, she had no doubt that he could definitely teach her a thing or two—and she'd more than enjoy returning the favor.

CHAPTER THIRTEEN

Marko

Pretty boy was nervous. Scratch that. Camacho was antsy. As his mother always said, poison ivy was the only thing that got a man more twitchy and itchy than a woman. The female who got Camacho all twitchy stood next to Isaac at the front of the B-Squad briefing room giving the rest of the team a rundown on Jarrod Fane, the Crest Society, and her niece Essie as if every single person in the room didn't already know it the whole story backwards and forwards.

Sure Tamara had given them the bare bones on the flight to the Indulgence Resort before they'd rescued Gidget from that crazy-ass drug-dealing bitch Yasmin Romanow, but he'd done some digging into Tamara's story after they'd returned. He wasn't the only one.

She might be brass tacks when it came to organization and logistics, but she didn't know jack about how hard it was to keep secrets in a place like the Devil's Dip Gym building.

The B-Squad worked together, they played together, they fought together, and they lived together on the second and third floors of the building like a hippie commune. Well, if that commune had access to enough firepower and know-how to take over a small country, anyway. But she'd been dead set on acting as if nothing was wrong and they'd let her. Looking back, that probably hadn't been the best plan.

Almost out of nowhere, a pair of pointy-toed black stilettos with a metal snake winding around the narrow, shiny four-inch heels landed on his thigh, jerking his attention away from the front of the room. His gaze traveled up from the wearer's feet to her long leather-encased legs to the jade green filmy tank top to Elisa Sharp's face as she sat in the chair next to him. She'd plopped down on the seat next to him right before the Isaac and Tamara show had started. Up until now she'd let him be. He'd known it wouldn't last. It never did.

The woman did love to toy with him as if he was an idiot boy fresh off the farm instead of the kind of highly sought-after scarred up and colorfully tattooed muscle with explosive expertise that mercenary companies from across the globe wanted. He'd been courted by the best and yet here he was in Fort Worth, being tormented by a pocket-sized badass who twisted the truth for a living.

His whole body itched and twitched and almost shuddered. Also, his dick got harder than the heels on her fuck-me shoes—not an unusual occurrence around the B-Squad's resident chameleon and con artist.

She raised one dark eyebrow and blew him a kiss.

It was a tease. They both knew it. He wasn't her type. She was small and beautiful and devious right to the core. He was big, lumbering and a mama's boy—okay, not really, but he and his mom did talk once a week. Family meant something to him. It always had. He'd started watching out for his mother and little sister the day his father went to prison for life and had never stopped. That wasn't going to change just because Duke, Lash, Keir, and Taz liked to bust his balls about it.

Unlike him, Elisa had lost her entire family when her dad died years ago. He'd asked her about it once and she'd told him family didn't matter. That was the instant he'd known that for as much as she turned him on, for as much as he wanted to fuck her silly, that was all it would ever be. Family meant everything to him. Always had. Always would.

Marko encircled Elisa's narrow ankles with one hand and lifted upward before she had the chance to rub against his cock, which was trying to go all Hulk on his jeans. He offered a silent apology to his dick and swung her legs away from him. Once she was clear, he released his hold, but not before he saw a knowing look cross her looks-like-an-angel face.

"Please don't say you're scared by little ol' me.," she whispered, leaning close enough into him that her tits pressed against his bicep.

He gulped past the rush of lust. "Right down to my bones."

"There's only one of those I'm interested in." She danced her fingertips up his thigh, stopping before things got interesting. "And it sure is interested in me."

He should remove her hand. Having her fingers that close to his cock while her tits were against his arm was detrimental to his higher functions. He knew it. She knew it. He kept his hands where they were.

"You're imagining that."

"Just like I imagine you're always watching me? That it's not by accident that we always end up sitting next to each other?"

"You sat down beside me," he responded.

"This time." She squeezed his thigh with her quick fingers before letting him go and nodding her chin at Isaac and Tamara. "Think they've fucked already?"

"I don't think about where Camacho's dick has been." Too many places to count was the answer to that.

"What about your dick?" Her hand was back, this time hovering over his thigh, the proximity almost as bad—in the best way possible—as her touch. "Where has it been lately?"

Not a question he'd be answering here. They were set off from the rest of the group, closest to the back wall and the door per usual and were whispering, but he'd be a fool to believe everyone in the room didn't have at least half an ear tuned into their discussion. Gossipy assholes.

"You're going to miss the briefing."

She snorted. "We both know the score. And what's going to have to happen next."

"Exfil and take down." The question was how they'd do it and how hard Tamara would fight it. She was smart, but she didn't trust anyone. Without that, you couldn't work in a team environment. Camacho had lone wolf disease so any mission involving him was already going to be a cluster fuck without adding in Tamara's stubborn streak.

"It's what we do—but not all we could be doing," she said, the look in her eyes as innocent as her meaning was downright dirty.

That's the way it was with her. You never knew what you were getting, what was a lie and what was true. He'd figured ignoring how she affected him was the way to go. Maybe it was time to change tactics and go on offense.

He turned in his seat, giving her the perfect view of a face that had seen too many fists to be called anything but ravaged. It wasn't enough, so he let his eyes go cold. Serious. Mercenary.

Her eyes widened and the vein in her neck jumped in response. This time he was the one who leaned in close, but not to whisper in her ear. He wanted to see her face.

"You looking for a quick, hard fuck, Elisa?"

"Always." Her breath was ragged, but she didn't flinch. She was too flinty for that.

God, the woman unnerved him, and damned if his dick didn't love it. Instead of answering, he turned his attention back to the front of the room. Tamara was finishing up with her spiel.

"Chicken." Elisa issued the one-word challenge with a soft chuckle.

He shook his head. "Smart."

"It's always the quiet ones that I really want to hear yell."

"You want to hear me to cry uncle?"

"That's not exactly the sexiest thing you could scream when you're buried inside me."

With that last shot, she stood and walked away swinging her narrow hips and giving him the perfect view of her pert, leather-clad ass as she crossed the room to where Vivi and Lexie stood. Typical. She wound him up and left him itching for more, which was exactly why he needed to stay the fuck away from her. Once he had a taste, he wasn't sure he'd be able to deny himself again—and there was nothing more dangerous than getting involved with a woman who lied for a living and liked it.

CHAPTER FOURTEEN

Isaac

Everyone in the room was getting restless. Isaac couldn't blame them. Vivi, Lexi and Elisa stood on one side of the room. They were a dangerous trio of investigative know-how, hacker can-do and flimflam artistry. Gidget was in attendance, sitting sandwiched between Taz and Bianca like a guarded treasure. Keir, Lash, and Duke were set up around a table littered with cards from an abandoned game of Spades between them. Only Marko sat by himself in the back of the room, dividing his attention between Tamara as she talked and Elisa across the room.

Even if Tamara didn't realize it, most of the B-Squad already knew more than a little of her story. Now they just wanted to get to the solution side of things. It sounded like a damn fine plan to him.

"So let me get this straight," Lexie said, her fingers flying across the keys of the laptop resting on top of a three-drawer filing cabinet. "Your sister married a cult leader who runs his own militia group. She managed to get out and was fighting for custody of her teenage daughter when she died. You got shared custody of Essie, but Fane owns almost all of the judges in the area, so you took off with the girl before he could win the court battle for full custody and force her to marry one of his toadies. She's hidden somewhere with someone you trust. Now Fane has found you, and it's only a matter of time until he grabs you and does whatever it takes to force Essie's location from you. Do I have that right?"

Tamara blanched but held her ground. "Pretty much."

"And you figured you'd wait until now to ask for help because...?" Keir asked, getting straight to the burr that had clearly forced its way under everyone's saddle, judging by the annoyed expressions on eight of the ten faces looking out at them. Taz and Bianca were the exceptions.

Tamara gripped her hands tight in front of her, but her voice remained steady. "Lash helped me set up security at the house and I figured that would be enough. I didn't want to involve anyone else in my mess more than I already had"

Vivi snorted. "Last night's almost-gunfight in front of our building pretty much took care of that."

Tamara turned crimson.

A responding protectiveness rushed through Isaac. He didn't mean to take a step in front of her, but he did. He couldn't stop himself. "That wasn't her fault."

"No one said it was, Camacho." A smile tugged at the edges of Bianca's lips. "So we need a three-pronged approach. We need to build a case against Fane, keep a twenty-four/seven watch on Tamara, and get Essie here so we can protect her."

"She's safe where she is," Tamara said, her knuckles turning white from her grip.

"No, she's not," Bianca said, her voice understanding. "If Fane found you, he can find Essie."

Like magic, even though it was just Lexie pushing a switch, a screen came down from the ceiling. On it was a photo of Jarrod Fane and a bio in bullet point form listing his age, known aliases, and closest advisors, along with a brief listing of law enforcement officials believed to be in his pocket.

Tamara's eyes widened for a fraction of a second before reality sank in. She might not have realized it up until that moment, but the B-Squad had taken her in as one of their own. Whether she thought she deserved it or not, she had a place with them, and that meant they'd help—even when she didn't ask.

"You're right." It cost Tamara to say those two words, but she hid it well —only the tightness around her mouth gave her away.

Taz nodded. "Go with Lexie and Vivi, they'll need all the information you can give them to work up a preliminary dossier so we can narrow down potential vulnerabilities."

"I can help," Isaac said. "I've been doing a little research on my own." Okay, a lot, but he didn't need to go into that in front of everyone.

"Imagine that," Lash said, not bothering to hide his smirk. "I suppose you think you'd be the best one to be her twenty-four/seven."

"Stop busting his chops, Lash," Bianca said, all business as she nailed Isaac to the floor with a piercing gaze. "This isn't like other freelance jobs. This is for one of our own. It's a team effort. No on goes lone wolf on this one."

Lone wolf? Is that what they wanted to call it? He didn't play well with others. He did what was right, not what he was told. It had cost him his rank. His livelihood. His brothers in arms. And if he had to go back and do it again, he wouldn't hesitate to pull the trigger. This wasn't Afghanistan, though, and the members of the B-Squad weren't a scared, mentally broken Marine with a gun to a four-year-old girl's head. In this specific instance, he could do the one thing he swore he'd never do again. Be a team player.

He nodded. "Understood."

Taz gave him a long, hard look, as if the former boxer was sizing him up before they stepped into the ring. "I sure hope so."

Heat flared in a primitive part of Isaac's brain, the one that responded to direct challenges with fists and firearms. It took a second, but he managed to push it back. Taz was just looking out for Tamara. The entire B-Squad was. They weren't the enemy. Jarrod Fane was. Still, the whole inquisition chapped his ass.

"If you're done lecturing me," he said with only the barest hint of a snarl. "Let's get this show on the road."

"Elisa and Marko, you'll tag-team as backup on this one," Bianca said, rattling off orders like she'd been born to run a team like this. "Get packed and be ready to go first thing in the morning. I'll call Jake Warrick with Absolute Security and tell him we need the jet back from Dry Creek, Nebraska ASAP. While you're getting Essie, the rest of us will monitor from here while we develop the case against Fane. Keir, you'll take lead on that. Pump your contacts for everything you've got, and I need it yesterday."

Isaac didn't wait for a dismissal. He had his orders. In a moment of complete non-verbal understanding, he and Tamara turned as a unit and strode across the room. Vivi and Lexie were already headed out into the hallway. He and Tamara followed out the door behind them. They'd taken a few steps into the hallway when Tamara slowed to a stop.

"What was that all about?" she asked.

He could tell her all about that night, peel back his skin and show her all the invisible scars that were still as jagged as they were in the heartbeat after he'd fired that kill shot. He could tell her. But he wouldn't. Some ugly was best left buried.

"I'm a man of mystery." He'd tried the good old boy grin, but it felt crooked on his face. So he did what he always did. He walked.

She curled her fingers around his forearm, stopping him. "No, you're not, you're—"

A muffled version of "Flight of the Valkyries" sounded from her purse. All the blood drained out of her face as she skipped rooting around for the phone and dumped it out in the middle of the hallway instead. She squatted down, shoving through the receipts, tubes of lipstick, and stray receipts until she retrieved her phone with trembling hands.

"Essie, what's wrong?" she asked, her voice pinched.

He couldn't hear the answer, but whatever it was made Tamara sink to the floor, her long hair covering her face.

CHAPTER FIFTEEN

Tamara

Blood rushed through her ears so fast that she could barely hear Essie's voice on the other end of the line of the burner phone. She'd given the number to Essie to call in case of emergency.

"Did you hear me, Aunt T? I think daddy found me."

Panicking—though tempting beyond words—wouldn't help. So Tamara sucked in a hard breath through her nostrils and let it out in one long exhale through her mouth. The roar in her ears quieted. *Better. Much better.* She could feel Isaac hovering above her, but every ounce of her attention needed to be focused on her niece.

"I heard you, Essie." Damn, she sounded totally calm and together for a woman sitting on her ass in the hallway on the verge of an anxiety attack. "Tell me everything."

"I was walking home from the library today and was a few blocks away from the house when I noticed a blue sedan going kinda slow. I figured it was probably a total creeper, so I stopped at one of the boutiques on Clifton Street and watched through the store window. One of the men in the car looked like a guy that used to hang around daddy."

This should not be happening. How in the hell had Jarrod managed to track Essie down? Tamara thought she'd been so careful. Then again, he'd lucked into finding her too. If he managed to get his hands on Essie, the bastard would use both instances as proof to his followers that God was on his side—if the man really was part of Jarrod's cult. It could be mistaken identity or a coincidence, but Tamara's twisted up gut didn't think so.

"The man in the car, was he part of the Crest Society?" she asked.

"No, but he did work for daddy. The kind of work that usually meant someone was in trouble."

"Are you sure it was him?"

"No, but I'm scared." There was more than just fear in Essie's voice. A fine thread of hysteria ran through each word.

Tamara eased herself back into a standing position, her back to the wall and Isaac in front of her, no doubt filling in the blanks of Essie's side of the conversation. "Where are you now?"

"After the sedan went by, I went into the store and out the back way. I ran through the alleys back to Albert's house. I didn't see the car again."

Good news—probably as good as they were going to get today. "Stay put. I'll be there as soon as I can. We're going to bring you to Fort Worth."

"But I thought hiding separately was the safest plan."

Tamara glanced up at Isaac. She really hated it when someone else was right, but she couldn't deny it in this case. "It was until your dad found me."

"Shit."

"Don't curse." It came out automatically, almost in her sister Amelia's voice.

"That's what you're worried about right now?" Essie's voice cracked over a stressed laugh.

"No. You know it's not." But the control freak in her demanded something not be out of whack, and if that meant enforcing her sister's rules on proper language then so be it. "I love you Essie."

"You too, Aunt T."

"Tell Albert to be on the lookout for us. You two stay safe and stay inside. Don't open up the doors for anyone. I'll be there tonight."

They said their goodbyes and Tamara hung up. She gathered up the guts of her purse that had spilled all over the floor until she could get her heart under control. Now that she was off the phone with Essie and free to freak out, her body was good and drunk on the speeding-pulse-shot-of-adrenaline cocktail.

"That didn't sound good," Isaac said, bending down to help her clean up.

"It's not. Essie thinks she spotted one of Jarrod's men."

Something dark and dangerous passed over his face, deepening the fine lines and hardening his jaw. "How soon can you leave?"

She dropped her favorite tube of Maraschino Red lipstick into her purse and stood up, nerves as steely as they were going to get until she had Essie safe. "Right now. My go-bag with the money in it is in my office."

"I'll tell the team the schedule just got moved up. We can't wait for the jet to get here. Meet me in the garage. We leave in five." He cupped her chin and tilted her face up. "Don't worry. We'll get Essie."

God she hoped he was right. "Tell the team to hurry and to pack for bear."

He grinned and brushed a quick kiss across her lips. "That's my girl."

She wasn't, but as she watched him sprint back into the briefing room part of her wished she could be.

Isaac

Twelve hours of driving time separated the Devil's Dip Gym and Hamilton, Colorado. Isaac was betting they could do it in ten. That meant instead of being comfortable in his truck, he was cramped inside a midnight blue Camaro with Fort Worth in the rearview and Amarillo out in the distance. Tamara sat in the passenger seat, her back ramrod straight and her hands clasped tight enough in her lap to make every knuckle in her fingers turn white. She'd been like that since they'd pulled out of the Devil's Dip Gym, and it was starting to make him twitchy.

"It's gonna be a long drive," he said, zipping around a family minivan with more dents than a back country road. "You might want to give your fingers a break."

She slowly turned her head to face him, her face set in a do-not-fuck-with-me expression. "Are you telling me to relax?"

"I guess so," he said, keeping his voice neutral enough to really tick her off.

"That's about the most ineffective way of getting me to do that."

"I don't know." He shrugged, loving the incensed spark in her blue eyes. "You're thinking about something other than what will happen if we don't get to Essie in time."

"That's your genius plan?" Her eyes narrowed until they were little more than slits. "Piss me off enough that I stop thinking about everything that could go wrong?"

"Pretty much."

She turned away from him with a huff, but her hands lay flat and relaxed in her lap. "Your plan sucks."

Texas passed in a brown and blue flash as the miles flew by. Country music filled the car with stories of good times, bad love, and everything in between. By the time they were headed toward New Mexico, the tension had mellowed into a comfortable silence, punctuated by music that grew ever scratchier as the highway went on. Time to use the mood to his advantage and do a little digging for information.

"Tell me about Essie."

Tamara kept her gaze on the scenery, resting her head against the seat. "She's smart. Everyone in the Crest Society homeschools their kids, but Amelia always found a way to teach Essie a little bit more than was expected. Most of the girls on the compound never get past middle school. Essie got her high school equivalency degree right before Amelia died."

Pride rang in her voice. She sounded like his mom whenever she started bragging about her kids, no matter how much it would embarrass him or his sisters.

"So what do you do with a super-smart sixteen year old when you're on the run?"

Smart kids sometimes meant more trouble than the dumb ones. They always figured out new ways to entertain themselves.

"Part of the reason I went to Albert for help is because Hamilton has a small liberal arts college that would be perfect for Essie to attend." She let out a bittersweet sigh. "I thought maybe next year, if we hadn't heard from her father, she could enroll."

It was a sweet—if totally naive—hope. "So much for that."

She snorted. "Exactly."

After that it was a fast-food drive thru, a fresh tank of gas just south of the Colorado state line, and small talk about music and movies. It was a straight shot north from the state line to Hamilton. The GPS predicted five and a half hours. At their current pace, they'd be there in four and a half. He lowered the sun visor and pushed it against the driver's side window so it helped block the setting sun coming in from the west.

"So what's the deal with this Albert guy?" he asked, holding the steering wheel a little tighter than necessary. "Is he an old boyfriend?"

"You mean you don't already know everything about him?" She said it jokingly, but the question had a punch to it. There was no way she was happy baring her secrets.

"Since I just found out about his existence today, no. I'm good, darlin' but I'm not that good. You managed to do a damn fine job of hiding Essie if I couldn't find her location until you gave it up."

"Fat lot of good it did. How in the hell did Jarrod manage to find her?"

"If he did." He had to say it even though that sixth sense that warned of something bad just around the corner was going nuts.

She brought her knees up to her chest and curled her arms around her legs, making herself a small, tight ball on the passenger seat. "My gut says the clock is ticking."

He got that, and he knew just how frustrating it was to know part of the equation but not the rest. Good thing they had nothing but time right now to unravel the mystery.

"Then let's figure it out." He tapped his thumbs on the steering wheel in time with the slow song playing on the radio. "If Fane sent out Wolczyk to sniff around your ex-husband who you hadn't seen for years, then he's leaving no stone unturned. Who is Albert to you? An old lover?"

That made her laugh. "Not a boyfriend that's for sure. Albert Glad-Lovatt is the secret weapon of every beauty queen who has ever won one of the major tiaras in the past thirty years. And I don't play for his team."

"He runs beauty pageants?"

"No." She shook her head. "He runs the girls."

He whipped his head around and gaped at her. Now that was not the answer he'd been expecting.

"Not like that," Tamara said, her eyes wide. "He's not a pimp. He's a pageant consultant— the best one there is. Even after I stopped doing pageants, we kept in touch. He's the closest thing I had to a mentor. When things got bad with my mom, I could always count on Albert."

Okay, that made sense. Perhaps what had kept Tamara safe all this time was the fact that she wasn't close to many people. As far as he could tell she'd only had Amelia, Albert, and Essie before landed with the B-Squad.

"Who knew you two were close?" he asked. Someone had to. If it had been an easy connection to make, he would have made it. That Fane may have gotten the drop on Isaac gnawed on him.

"My mom, who I haven't spoken with in years. A few of the girls from the pageants, most of whom I'm not in touch with. The others, it's only enough to make small talk at parties where we cross paths. No one else. Not even Taz."

"Albert didn't come to the wedding?"

"Taz and I eloped. It seemed very romantic at the time."

"And now?" He didn't mean to hold his breath, he just couldn't help it. What she said next mattered.

Tamara sighed and laid her cheek on top of her kneecap. "It seems like I was running away as fast as I could."

The air whooshed out of him and his shoulders eased down. "We're all guilty of that sometimes."

"Oh yeah? What are you running from?" she asked. "What was that whole pissing contest about following orders during the meeting?"

He should have known she wouldn't let it go. She wasn't the type. Her bulldog attitude was one of the things he liked about her best, but that didn't mean he wanted his past to be the bone she wouldn't let go of. Silence thickened the atmosphere inside the Camaro as the sun-parched scenery of southeast Colorado flew past. He opened his mouth to tell her in no uncertain terms to mind her own business, but that's not what came out.

"I met Lash in the Marine Corps. We were in the same unit until he rotated back to the states and got out. His replacement was...different."

"What do you mean?"

How to describe Mitchum. Corn-fed? In over his head? Too green to know better than to believe the bullshit?

"The kids was young and on his third deployment."

Tamara let out a low whistle and unfolded her legs, pivoting in her seat so she faced him. "Damn, that's a lot."

He nodded. "Especially for someone who may not have been all that mentally healthy to begin with."

The signs had been there, but no one wanted to see them. Even when

Isaac had pointed them out to his superiors, their eyes wouldn't see the cracks that had been growing every day.

"The kid couldn't hack it. He needed to rotate back stateside. I made the recommendation. My commander disagreed. The kid stayed in." Isaac clenched his jaw and watched the semi-trucks up ahead jockey for position on the interstate. "One day, we were out as part of the whole hearts and minds effort at a local village. The kid snapped, grabbed a four-year-old girl, and put a gun to her head. We tried to talk him down. The girl was crying. Her mother was screaming. Her father was begging us to do something— anything. My commander was ordering everyone not to fire. The kid locked eyes with me and I knew. That was it for him. He was done. He wasn't ever going to see home again and he didn't want to. He thought that was his best way out. If he had to take that little girl with him to make it happen, so be it. I couldn't let that happen. I fired. Took him out."

Where there should have been chaos there was only shock followed by a world of shit raining down on him.

"Did they court martial you?"

"There was a reporter embedded with us that day." Who'd have ever thought the skinny little puke would have been his saving grace? "He saw the whole thing. They couldn't court martial me without making a shitty situation even worse in the national media. Still, they wanted me out for not following orders, and I went."

"Isaac, I'm sorry," her voice was thick with sincerity.

One glance over and he could confirm it, but he couldn't risk it. He was in too deep with her already.

"I'm not."

He'd come home and hadn't known what to do with his life until Lash brought up the idea of freelance investigation. Since Isaac had absolutely no interest in ever working in a team environment with some asshole giving orders again, it had been the perfect solution, —although it didn't explain why he spent so much time working overflow cases for the B-Squad. Unwilling to go down that path, he turned up the radio and let the country singer belt it out.

Tamara

The air was thinner in Hamilton. Isaac parked the car across the street from Albert's two-story grey and white Victorian house with the wrought iron fence surrounding the front yard. It had been dark for several hours by the time they got to the small town in the Rocky Mountain foothills. Tamara hadn't wanted to risk calling the house, so she'd spent the last several, very quiet hours in the car doing breathing exercises and telling herself everything was going to be all right.

Seeing the bright blaze of Albert's porch light did more to calm her down than all the mantras she'd muttered under her breath.

She reached for the door, but Isaac clapped a hand down on her forearm.

"Give it a second," he said, his gaze going from house to house pausing to take in each car parked on the street and every person going for their nightly stroll.

It took forever—or at least it felt that way.

Being this close and not rushing in was making her fingers twitch. "The cars are empty. The old lady picked up her yappy dog's poop and went back inside. Can we go in now?"

He nodded and opened his door. "Wait for a second before you approach the house."

Frustration ate away at her, but she stepped out of the car and waited while he went around to the trunk. She couldn't see what was going on once he'd opened it, but when he closed it, he dropped both of their go bags to the ground and then squatted down to start fiddling with the license plate holder. After a minute, he grabbed the bags and strode past her. His dress shirt was left unbuttoned over a T-shirt was open, giving her a view of the Glock secured in his shoulder holster. Isaac stopped at the front of the car where he swapped the front Texas license plate out with one from Colorado. He put the Texas plate into his go bag, zipped it closed and stood up, holding both bags.

"Ready?" he asked.

She nodded and took her bag. That left his right hand free for the Glock. She didn't have a gun. The way her nerves were doing the cha-cha she didn't really trust herself with one right now.

Isaac led the way across the street and up to the front door. When he knocked, it swung slowly open.

Panic flared to life and she rushed forward. Isaac's strong arm blocked her.

"Stay behind me and stay low," he whispered, pushing her behind his body.

"Essie." Her heart nearly beat out of her chest. "Albert."

"They're going to be fine," he said over his shoulder before making his way into the house, gun drawn and duffle bag abandoned on the porch.

Holding onto her sanity enough to heed the logic of his words took everything she had—but she did it, leaving her bag and following him through the dark house. It wasn't a fast or loud process. He was as silent as she'd ever seen him as he cleared each area on their march back to the sole room with a light on. It shined through the space between the swinging kitchen door and the hardwood floor.

Bile rose in her throat. Part of her didn't want to know what was beyond that door. Whatever it was, it wouldn't be good. Not for Essie. Not for Albert.

Issac held out a hand, palm facing her. He pointed at her, then the floor.

Stay. Yeah, that wasn't going to happen. He narrowed his eyes. She shook her head. Just because she was scared at what they'd find behind door number one didn't mean she wasn't going in.

A low, pitiful moan sounded from behind the door. "They're gone. They left hours ago."

Albert!

Before Isaac could stop her, she burst through the door and into the bright kitchen. Albert sat duct taped to a chair in the middle of the room, a white piece of paper fastened to his blood-splattered shirt. His usually perfectly coiffed white hair was sticking up in places and a purple bruise covered half his face. Her gut clenched and tears pricked her eyes. She'd brought this here. She'd put one of the few people in the world who she counted as a friend in danger.

"Are you okay? Is anything broken," she asked as she sprinted to his side, kneeling so she could tear at the tape with her fingers. "Where's Essie?"

Isaac handed her a pair of scissors he'd unearthed from somewhere and she started snipping at the tape on one side while he went to work slicing with a knife on the other.

"Two men took her," Albert said, his words muffled by the swelling on his bottom lip. "I tried to stop them but I couldn't. I'm so sorry."

"No. I am." She ripped the tape free, glad Albert was such a firm believer in body waxing. "I never should have forced you into this position."

"Like anyone could make me do anything, Chippy." Albert gave her the imperious smirk he always wore when he used his pet name for her, but his obvious wince ruined the effect. "They left you a message."

Her mentor ripped off the white paper attached to his shirt and handed it to her. The warning was printed in big block letters in black marker. The paper shook in her hands, but not enough that she couldn't make out the message.

LET HER GO WHILE YOU'RE STILL BREATHING.

The bastard thought she'd give up. That she'd just let him have Essie to save her own skin. He was wrong. Jarrod Fane couldn't be more wrong if he'd declared the sun rose in the West—and he was going to pay for it.

"They've gotta be on their way back to Redfin for judgement and then her wedding, just like he planned all along." Just saying the words out loud made her want to throw up.

Isaac took the note from her, read it and crumpled it in his fist. "I'll have Elisa and Marko reroute the jet to Idaho, with a stop here to get us."

That wouldn't be until morning. It wasn't acceptable. God knew what Essie was going through right now. How scared she must be.

"They have a head start on us," she said. "We need to be on the road now."

"No." Isaac holstered his gun and took out his cell phone. "What we need is time to develop a plan—not a lot but until morning should do. Even if we were to take off now, by the time we caught up with them Essie would already be inside the Crest Society compound, where every resident is armed, loyal to Fane, and probably under orders to shoot you upon sight. We have to figure out a way to get inside, get her, and get out before Fane knows what the hell is going on. If we do this wrong, everyone will pay the price."

Waiting wasn't her thing, but he was right--and Jarrod was about to find out just what a mistake he'd made.

CHAPTER SIXTEEN

Isaac

Because he worked mostly on his own, Isaac had never needed an encrypted phone before. Sitting in the trashed remains of Albert's kitchen, he offered up a grateful thank you to Bianca for insisting he take one with him before hitting the road. He hit the speaker button and dialed.

Marko answered on the first ring. "We're both here. Talk."

This was usually when Isaac would make some smart ass remark about the other man being a real chatterbox, but nothing about tonight was normal. "There's been a development."

"Shit," Elisa muttered.

That pretty much summed up Isaac's view on everything that had happened since the high point of waking up next to Tamara. By the time he'd brought Marko and Elisa up to speed about what they'd found in Hamilton, Tamara had wandered back into the kitchen to throw a wad of duct tape into the garbage. Up on the second floor, a shower kicked on. He couldn't blame Albert for wanting to wash off the last few hours under scalding hot water.

Tamara's shoulders were curved forward, her long blonde hair tucked behind her ears, her eyes downcast. Weary. His girl looked worn out and ready for a month of sleep. He couldn't blame her. It was a lot to take.

"We need you two to meet us up in Redfin," he said keeping his attention on Tamara as she sat down across from him. "We're headed out before first light. It's a five and a half hour drive."

"The jet will be back at seven tomorrow morning. That'll give us time for a refill and quick restock." Marko's voice came in clear through the phone laid in the middle of the wood table. "We can be there by nine at the latest."

"Is Tamara there?" Elisa asked.

She straightened up in her chair. "I'm here."

"Tell us about the compound," Marko said.

Tamara sighed and her shoulders dipped farther forward. "It's large. Fenced. Guarded at the gate and at locations around the perimeter. Each family has their own mini-compound situated in a ring just inside the perimeter. Essie will be at Jarrod's quarters, which is smack dab in the middle of everything."

"That confirms the information we got from the Feds," Marko said.

Isaac's head snapped up. Now that was news. Could be good news. Could be bad. "The Feds are involved?"

Elisa's soft laugh filtered out of the phone. "Let's just say they already had an interest. Seems Fane hasn't always followed the law when acquiring his guns, or with what he's got stocked inside the armory. If we can bring back a firsthand account to back that up, they'd be mighty appreciative."

"What do you mean firsthand?" he asked. A regular exile mission had enough chances to go sideways without adding a little lookie-lou for the Feds.

"Marko and I go in as possible recruits to check the place out," Elisa said, as if gathering first-person intel on a cult that operated like a militia on crack wasn't a big deal.

Tamara shook her head as if Marko and Elisa could see her. "Jarrod will never fall for that."

"He will when our covers have been in place for months," Elisa said. "Did you really think we've been sitting back without plans A through Z for a possible operation against this dickwad? You both know how it works with B-Squad. We protect our own—even if they don't want the help."

Tamara looked at Isaac, her blue eyes shining. She wasn't crying, but the tip of her nose had turned red and her lips were pursed tight despite the tremble in her chin. He never thought he'd see her speechless but this was it. The ice princess had finally melted. The urge to gather her in his arms was overwhelming. While most women would welcome the touch, he knew it was the wrong move with Tamara. That veneer of frigid untouchability was all that was keeping her together at the moment. He wouldn't take that away from her.

"I don't know what to say," she said, her voice shaky.

"Nothing to say," Marko replied. "It's just the way it is."

"Thank you."

"Let's not get mushy," Elisa said. "I don't do mushy."

Tamara wiped her cheek with the back of her hand. Isaac kept his hands flat on the table and pretended not to notice.

"We'll rendezvous at the diner next to the Idaho Inn before Elisa and I visit the compound," Marko said. "It's in Causewell, thirty miles from

Redfin. Far enough to be outside Fane's direct influence, but use stage one precautions, just in case. No direct contact after this—everything goes through Bianca at headquarters. Your reservation for the motel is under Pat and Penny Hargrove. Your cover is that you're tourists. Be sure to look the part."

A small smile tugged at one side of Tamara's mouth. "Don't worry, we have a secret weapon in the makeover department."

Isaac didn't know what exactly that meant, but he had a really bad feeling he was about to find out. The only thing that kept him from bolting was the woman sitting across from him. Tamara had pulled back from the edge of falling apart. Damn, she was impressive.

Tamara

Albert could do a makeover in his sleep. A makeunder? That required reinforcements.

"I had to guess your size, Mr. Camacho," he said handing Isaac a plastic bag emblazoned with Hamilton University's logo on it, along with a second bag from a discount store. "If these don't fit let me know and I'll send Skye back again."

Albert hadn't said so, but there was no missing that Skye was a pageant champion in the making. She was tall, confident, and had a big smile no matter what—although it had shaken when she'd spotted Albert's bruised up face. If she didn't have at least five major sashes framed on her wall already, Tamara would eat the brand-new hot pink GO BULLDOGS! T-shirt Albert had handed her.

"Don't make that face." He waved his hand in a circular motion in her general direction. "You'll get wrinkles."

She shook her head. Somethings never changed. "Albert, I'm retired. I'm allowed to get wrinkles."

He arched an eyebrow at her, but it took work. Must be too soon after his last Botox treatment. Some people smoked. Some people ate an entire bag of Oreos in one sitting. Albert's addiction was perfect skin no matter what. Hell, who was she to judge? She was on the run from a megalomaniac, and anyway Albert was the best friend a washed-up beauty queen could ever have.

He pivoted on his bare feet and marched toward the bathroom. "Young lady, you're coming with me. You're going to become a brunette, but don't worry. It's only temporary."

She started to follow but hesitated before walking out of the living room. Isaac stood in the middle of the room looking totally out of place in the room decorated in pageant memorabilia, from the chandelier with its tiny light-up tiaras to the framed covers of Pageant Monthly. With his worn cowboy boots and painted-on jeans, he looked ridiculous in Albert's living room...and close enough to perfect to make her breath catch.

"Do you think it's me?" He held up the neon green T-shirt with a growling bulldog on the front.

She laughed. "I don't think that shirt is anyone."

"Aw hell," he muttered as he pawed through the plastic bag. "There's boat shoes in here."

The last time she'd seen him out of his cowboy boots, they were both getting naked as fast as humanly possible. Heat sizzled its way up from her belly at the memory. With all that had gone on, thinking about Isaac naked and buried inside her should be the last thing she should be thinking about. That she couldn't help but play that mental movie just went to show how selfish she was. Albert, Isaac, the B-Squad, even Skye, who she'd barely set eyes on—they were all coming to her rescue. The least she could do was not behave like a hormonal teenager with her first crush.

"I gotta go." The fact that she didn't want to go scared her enough to get her feet moving.

He nodded and shoved his long fingers through his dark hair. "Try to get a couple hours of sleep. We're heading out before dawn."

Chicken that she was, Tamara scurried out of the room like it had just caught fire.

Thirty minutes later she was sitting on the edge of Albert's garden tub, her hair slick with brown semi-permanent dye.

"Color from a box." Albert made a series of tsk-tsk noises and adjusted the plastic hair cap covering her wet strands. "It makes my heart hurt."

"Do you remember when I tried to dye it myself a week before the Miss Crystal Dream pageant?" Disaster didn't cover it. Her mother had been too mad to snipe at her—a first.

"Blue." Albert laughed, a deeper sound than one would expect from the tall, thin man in white who always managed to look pristine, even now with half his face bruised up. "A beauty queen with blue hair. Thank God for emergency hair stylists."

The stylist had had to strip the color out of her hair and start fresh. She'd smelled bleach in her sleep for weeks afterward. "I'd thought it would be more pastel blue and less electric blue."

He sat down on the vanity chair opposite her, his unlined face peaceful. "Things so seldom go exactly the way we plan."

Wasn't that the story of her life. She was supposed to be a trophy wife. She'd gotten close. She'd married Taz, but he hadn't been on the hunt for a trophy wife. He hadn't realized it, but he'd been looking for love, and she wasn't made for that kind of commitment. And now she knew why. Because it hurt—not just her, but everyone around her.

"Albert, I'm so sorry about this. I never should have involved you."

"Involved me? I do believe you fought me tooth and acrylic nail to leave

Essie here while you went down to Fort Worth."

"So I could blackmail Taz. Another brilliant plan."

"Not your best, I'll agree, but you were desperate and backed into a corner."

"And look how much bigger of a mess I've made." Albert was hurt. Isaac had almost been dragged into a gunfight. Essie was right back where she'd started. "I should have just taken Essie to another country and lived under a fake name."

"You knew as soon as you got Essie out of Redfin that Jarrod would never give up until he took her back. That's the real reason you went to Fort Worth with that cockamamie plan to get a million dollars from your ex-husband. Because you don't know how to just ask for help."

Was he right? Had she just been looking for an excuse to ask for help? She'd like to have said no, but there was more than a nugget of truth to what he said. Asking for help had never been on her list of talents. Hell, she'd been raised to believe that it did nothing but make you vulnerable to other people. In reality, it just brought trouble to innocent people's doors.

She clasped her hands together as tightly as she could, the pain helping to center her. "I asked for your help, and look what happened."

Albert shrugged his shoulders as if a home invasion, beating, and kidnapping were all part of his normal routine. "I knew the risks going in, and I believed it was worth it. I still do."

"Thank you." The words were inadequate, but what else could she say? Just getting that out was hard enough with the emotion clogging her throat.

"It's what mentors do. We help you be the best you can be." The timer on his phone went off in a series of quick beeps. He tapped the screen, stood, and crossed over to her. "Speaking of which, tell me about Mr. Tall, Dark, and Dashing."

"I don't know where to start." And she didn't. It was like there was more to him than she could put into words.

He turned on the water and removed her plastic cap. "I'd suggest with the belt buckle."

Her cheeks blazed. "Albert!"

He gently pushed her shoulders back so her head was over the tub and used the hand-held shower head rinse her hair clean. "Oh, come on, I can tell by the way you look at each other that you already have."

She closed her eyes to keep out the stray spray of water, but that only made picturing Isaac naked and pressed against the wall easier. In half a heartbeat she could taste him, hear his moan, feel the tremble in his thighs as she'd sucked him deep. That was bad enough. What had her gritting her teeth as water sluiced through her hair was the heavy sense of rightness that wrapped itself around her, as warm and solid as the softest fur.

"He's a distraction." One she couldn't afford.

Albert snorted. "The kind that blazes a route across the country to help rescue Essie, a girl he's never met and has no ties to?"

"He's got a hero complex." A crude description for the bone-deep sense of honor he tried to hide under layers of cheap charm and unceasing flirting. His story about the Marine said it all. He didn't do what was easy. Isaac Camacho always did what was right.

"And you, my dear, have always seen yourself as the villain you never were." He turned the water off and squeezed the water from her hair. "Sounds to me like you're a match made in heaven."

She sat up and took the towel Albert offered to wipe the stray drops of water from her face, letting her damp hair hang like a curtain down her back while she gathered her icy reserves.

She handed back the towel, trying for a smile that almost passed for real. "You're a romantic."

"You don't look this good at 68 unless you believe in a little magic, darling." His words were light, but weariness invaded his eyes and stayed for a few seconds before he chased it away with a pageant-worthy fake smile of his own. "Now come on, time to blow dry. Then it's off to curl up with your white knight for a few hours of beauty sleep."

It was pretty to think so, but no one knew better than she exactly what kind of person she deserved, and it sure wasn't Isaac. She was a bitch. A gold digger. A girl who'd grown up to become exactly the kind of woman her mother had trained her to be. Isaac deserved much better than her.

Isaac

Waking up at three a.m. hurt a lot more than already being awake at three a.m., but it wasn't the alarm that forced Isaac's eyes open. It was the woman crying on the other side of the Jack-and-Jill bathroom door.

Crying was the wrong word. More like whatever people called that herky-jerky breathing thing women did when they were trying to cry quietly. The first time his sister Leah had her heart stomped on in high school, she'd shut herself in her bedroom and made that sound for hours.

He sat up and whipped off the covers. His feet sank into the thick carpet when he stood up, wearing only his boxers. There was a line of light coming out from under the door. He never made the conscious decision to ask her what was the matter, he just ended up across the room with his palm pressed against the door.

"Tamara, are you okay?"

"I'm fine," her voice was high, strained. "Sorry if I woke you."

He tried the knob. It was locked. "Let me in."

"I'm going to the bathroom." The words came out too shaky to be truth.

"Liar."

"I just need to get myself together." Her voice broke on the last word, but she sounded closer.

He tried the knob again. It was a simple turn lock, the kind he could have popped half drunk and totally blind, but breaking in wasn't the best plan. "Let me in."

"I don't—"

"Darlin', just let me in."

The lock clicked. He exhaled the breath he'd been holding and turned the knob. The door swung open, revealing the narrow bathroom with a bath/shower combo on the right side, a sink and toilet on the left, and the door that lead to Tamara's room directly across from the door leading to his. Tamara stood at the sink, her trembling shoulders hunched and her face turned away from him. She wore an oversized T-shirt and not much—if anything—else. Her formerly blonde hair was mousy brown and tied into the tight bun at the top of her head. She clutched a toothbrush in one hand and the other was curled into a fist.

The ice queen was gone, all her frozen defensive structures melted. Whatever had gone wrong now had peeled away everything, leaving only the vulnerable core. She'd hate to be seen like this, but she'd let him in anyway. Every protective instinct he had risen to the forefront at her show of trust in him, but it was more than that, something he couldn't put a name to. Not yet. Whatever had happened now to make her break down like this, he swore he'd find a way to make it right.

"What else happened?"

"Else?" She stayed turned away from him, but her body vibrated with tension. "I don't know if I could stand if something else bad happened to someone because of me."

He strode across the bathroom and pulled her into his arms. She fit so perfectly there, like he'd been made to curl himself around her and keep her safe, to be the one who would always be there.

She sank into him, resting her damp cheek against his bare chest. At that moment, he couldn't wait to meet Jarrod Fane face to face so he could rip him apart, one appendage at a time. He'd take it slow, extend the pain as long as possible, and it still wouldn't be enough to make up for this.

Isaac dipped his head down and brushed a kiss across her temple, whispered against her hair that it would be all right. He'd do whatever it took to make sure of that.

He hooked a finger under her chin and tilted her head up so he could look into her face as he made that promise to her, but the moment she looked up at him with tears glittering in her eyes, the words deserted him. All he meant to do was comfort her, let her know she wasn't alone. A soft kiss on the forehead. A brief touch on her cheek. By the time he got to her lips, she was on her tiptoes clinging to him, her tears dry and her mouth hungry for all he could give.

She opened beneath him and he deepened the kiss, relishing the feel of her response and the sound of her muffled moan as he licked, sucked, and tasted her. It wasn't a nice kiss. It wasn't meant to comfort her—not anymore. It had turned into that play for control, for dominance in a game they'd been playing since he brought her that glass of wine at Taz and Bianca's engagement party. He fisted her T-shirt in one hand, pulling it higher as his free hand went lower and cupped her firm ass. He held her close against his fast-hardening cock and she arched against him, a plaintive groan escaping her lips as her mouth slipped away from his. Her hands slid up between their bodies, so hot and hungry for more, but instead of a caress, she planted a palm above his heart and pushed back.

She didn't stop moving until there was half a bathroom between them. "I can't do this."

He took a step toward her. "I know the timing is wrong." To put it mildly. The middle of a mission wasn't exactly the ideal time to have more than a no-strings-attached adrenaline fuck, and whatever was going on between them was far from that.

"It's not the timing." There wasn't any fire in her words, no heat in her eyes. She'd gone stone cold.

Realization stopped him in his tracks. "It's me."

Her only response was silence. The kind that made the air thick and heavy enough to sock you in the gut and leave you breathless. It wasn't an unfamiliar feeling. He'd experienced the same thing in the moments after he'd pulled the trigger in Afghanistan, after he realized his Corps wouldn't back him up. After he'd woken up that first morning as a man without a mission or a tribe. He'd sworn he'd never be in that position again. He'd never again need that camaraderie, that sense of belonging. Tamara's dismissal shouldn't have the same emotional punch—but it did.

"We leave in ten, darlin'." This time he made sure that last word came out more of a curse than an endearment.

She nodded, her eyes guarded.

Even as he turned away, the urge to reach out to her, pull her close and reignite her icy fire, grabbed him by the throat and squeezed tight. It was all he could do to put one foot in front of the other and get the fuck out of the bathroom before he lost the fight.

She'd pulled the pin on whatever had been developing between them. He wasn't about to burn up in the explosion. Instead, he'd focus on the mission, rescue Essie, and take the long way back to Fort Worth. Alone.

CHAPTER SEVENTEEN

Tamara

Five hours after giving Albert a long hug goodbye, Tamara unbuckled her seatbelt, opened the Camaro's passenger door and stepped out into the gravel parking lot of The Idaho Inn. The short, squat building's best days had occurred a decade or two back. There was peeling paint, crooked shutters, and a buzzing neon "vacancy" sign hanging in the office window. Sharing the gravel lot was a sad-looking diner with two beat-up trucks parked in front.

The whole place looked a relaxing oasis after the world's most tension-filled road trip. It hadn't been pleasant but it needed to be done. When Isaac had kissed her, the whole world had gone sideways, and she was barely holding on as it was. She had to stick with what she'd told herself the moment she'd looked up at Isaac at Taz and Bianca's engagement party. Men were off the menu. Her plate was full enough already. All her focus had to be on rescuing Essie.

Isaac slammed the driver's side door and circled around the back of the muscle car to her side. He didn't touch her. He didn't need to. She would have known he was there if she'd been blindfolded and hog-tied. She could add that to the list of reasons why she'd had to end that kiss last night, because if it had gone on any longer, she wouldn't have been able to back away, and Isaac deserved better than someone like her.

He stopped next to her and rested his hand on the small of her back, leading her toward the diner. The electric awareness of him sizzled up her arm as they walked across the parking lot, and her pulse sped up even as she tried to ignore it. No doubt, from a distance they looked like an average married couple on vacation, but up close there was no way to miss the fact that Isaac's flirty smile didn't reach his eyes.

"Let's grab a bite before checking in," he said.

"Sounds great," she said, playing her part. "I'm starving."

The town of Causewell was 30 miles from Redfin, but that didn't mean Jarrod didn't have ears here. They'd stick to the plan Isaac had outlined before going radio silent for the rest of the trip.

A little bell tinkled when Isaac opened the glass door, and a blast of cool air carrying the smell of bacon grease swirled around them. She missed Marko and Elisa at first glance, but Isaac guided her to a booth in the corner next to one occupied by a man in overalls and a boy in a baggy T-shirt and ball cap pulled down low. It wasn't until the boy winked at her as she slid across the seat in her booth that she realized it was Elisa. Even then, it was hard to align the real Elisa, with her curves and perfect skin, with the sullen teen with his peach-fuzz mustache and pock-marked face.

Isaac sat with his back to them and picked up the laminated menu. "What looks good?"

Tamara was trying to make sense of it all in her head when Marko answered.

"We'll be at your grandmother's soon, Tony," he said in a voice softer than his usual gruff bass. "We'll be staying overnight, so don't let me forget to call Mama B to let her know we made it in okay. She'll be mighty teed off if we forget."

"Whatever," Elisa said with the bored insolence that teenagers seemed to have in abundance.

Tamara knew from reading mission reports that Mama B was Bianca. The code name and disguises were all part of stage one precautions, she knew, but it all seemed a little over the top...right up until their waiter stopped at their table. He was an older man who looked like a grandpa from one of Norman Rockwell's paintings, except for the bright red intertwined C and S—The Crest Society's logo—on the inside of his wrist. Tamara's eyes widened with surprise before she dropped her gaze as he filled her coffee mug.

"What can I get you folks?" the waiter asked.

She managed to mumble nothing for her while Isaac ordered half the menu for himself. By the time the waiter left with their order, Marko and Elisa were gone. The plan was in motion, even if it was a total fucking mystery to her. As soon as she got Isaac alone in the motel room, she was going to get every little detail he'd obviously failed to tell her when he'd gone into full on silent mode in the car.

CHAPTER EIGHTEEN

Marko

The Crest Society's compound reminded Marko of the Pentagon. It had the same five-sided shape with a protected center, and no doubt a person's level of importance grew higher the farther in you went. He and Elisa hadn't even made it into the outer layer before being stopped by security and ordered to park the extended-cab truck registered to one Mark Ryan. Marko had complied, gotten out, and offered his fake ID before telling the security guards he had an appointment. They'd called it in. He'd nodded to Elisa and she'd gotten out of the truck, walked over, and stopped three steps behind him. Glancing back wasn't the best idea, but he couldn't help it. His gaze always seemed to go right to her no matter what.

Seeing Elisa with her eyes downcast and as silent as a good, submissive wife should be didn't just seem wrong to Marko—it had his fingers itching to unwind the long rope of temporarily auburn hair she'd wound around her head in some kind of braid and let the real Elisa out. That wasn't going to happen though, so he shoved his hands into the pockets of his cargo pants to stop himself from reaching out to her and turned back around.

The armed guards standing in front of the compound's entrance with their hands resting on the butts of their holstered nine millimeters weren't important. They were cannon fodder. The man striding through the open gate, he was important. Tall and lanky, he moved like a man confident that the seas would part if he wished it. Marko didn't spot a gun or any obvious bulges denoting a concealed carry, but that didn't mean the man wasn't as dangerous as a bear just out of hibernation.

"Mr. Ryan. It's good to finally meet you in person." Seth Wainger held out his hand, completely ignoring Elisa as if she wasn't any more important than a family pet.

It was a typical move from one of the Crest Society's male members, but it still pissed Marko off. He shook Fane's second-in-command's hand, squeezing harder than necessary but not nearly as much as he wanted. For as long as he could remember, he'd fucking hated assholes who could only make themselves feel better by making others feel worse. Self-worth wasn't a zero sum game. Of course, bullies never understood that. The dumb fucks.

"I second that," Marko said, turning his body so Elisa was cut off from consideration and the conversation.

He was here. He had a part to play. He'd swallow past the sour taste and be just the kind of douchebag his mother would cuff hard on the back of the head and his little sister, Gillie, would goad into insanity.

Wainger crossed his arms over his narrow chest and tipped his head back toward the guards. "The welcome may be a little much, but we never know when the government will try one of their fishing expeditions."

"Happen a lot?" Marko asked, keeping his tone neutral.

The other man shrugged. "Often enough."

According to the information Keir had turned up, six times in as many months. "You'd think they'd get the message."

"Amen to that." He gestured toward the gate. "Let's go in. I can show you around a bit. Mr. Fane is in a meeting, but he'll track us down as soon as he's free. I know he's anxious to meet you."

More like he was anxious to meet Mark Ryan's fictitious bank account. "And I him." He paused for second. "What about my wife?"

Wainger's attention didn't even flicker to Elisa in her ankle-length dress with full sleeves and a high neckline. "We have a women's retreat here where the wives and soon-to-be wives bake, sew, and do their outside of the home chores."

"Sounds perfect." If he'd been looking to torture Elisa.

"Keith." One of the guards stepped forward. "Have one of the women take…" He looked to Marko, obviously pausing for him to fill in the blank.

Marko knew just what to say to a bunch of dickless wonders who were so scared of women they had to take away every bit of autonomy they had. "Mrs. Mark Ryan."

Approval made Wainger's beady little eyes gleam. "Exactly. Have one of the women take Mrs. Mark Ryan to the women's retreat while I give Mark the full tour."

Marko walked through the open gate with Wainger without even a look back at Elisa. If it had been any other woman on the B-Squad, he'd be worried about getting pelted in the back of the head with a rock, or worse, for treating her so poorly. It wasn't that Elisa was submissive. It wasn't that she didn't care. It was that no one lost themselves in a con role like she did. It was the coolest and scariest thing he'd ever seen, and it made him curious as hell to know the woman she was when she wasn't playing a role.

CHAPTER NINETEEN

Isaac

The ice queen had returned and Isaac didn't give three shits. He'd taken his time at the diner, filling up on eggs, real bacon, hash browns, and more while she nursed her cup of coffee like it was ninety percent moonshine. By the time he put a wad of cash on the table that would cover the meal and a decent tip, the disdain in her eyes had gone from frosty to glacial to downright arctic-tundra-on-the-winter-solstice cold.

"Ready to go, darlin'?" He was too pissed to care that he was being a petty asshole.

She narrowed her eyes and slid out of the booth. "Don't call me that."

"Do you prefer wifey?" he asked, giving a quick wave to the waiter, a Crest Society lookout judging by his tattoo and the way he hadn't taken his eyes off him and Tamara since they walked in.

The waiter gave him a commiserating look as Isaac opened the diner's door for his fake bride.

"I'd prefer you tell me what the fuck is going on," she said, her voice clipped and cold.

"Why, we're on the road trip from hell and fighting like two alley cats with their tails tied together."

An answer and a warning. She wasn't a field operative and she was pissed, but that didn't excuse fucking up this operation by asking questions that were better left until they were alone. Tamara cut him a glare that showed all the fire underneath that frigid facade of hers before stalking past him. He barely made it to the door before she did to hold it open for her like his mama had taught him. Tamara barely acknowledged the gesture as she stalked past, her chin high and her ass just as abso-fucking-lutely perfect

105

as it was two nights ago when he'd cupped it and driven deep into her while she writhed in ecstasy underneath him.

He followed her out into the bright sunshine, across the gravel parking lot, and into the Idaho Inn's lobby. Sure, he could have outtalked her easily, but the view wouldn't have been nearly as good, and he had enough testosterone in him to appreciate that fact even if he was an eight on the ten-point-pissed-off scale.

The tiny lobby was cramped and in about as good condition as the rest of the motel. An older woman with sun-dried skin and cast iron gray hair sat behind the desk.

Isaac put on his tourist voice. "Hi there. We have reservations under Pat Hargrove." He laid enough cash for the room on the counter.

The woman didn't blink at the money or ask for ID. Instead, she slid the registration log toward him. "Sign here." When he did, she turned and grabbed a pair of keys from the ten or so hanging on the peg board behind the desk. "Room twenty-three. It's around the corner at the end."

He scrawled "Pat Hargrove" on the log, took the keys, and strolled out the door. Tamara would follow. The stubborn woman wanted answers more than she wanted to make a stink. He wasn't wrong. She marched alongside when he grabbed their duffle bags from the car—although she snagged hers and slung it over her arm—and on to the room.

It was gloomy inside, even more so when he shut the door and locked it behind them. His first instinct was the open the shades, but he wasn't sure he wanted a better look at the room than the dim light from the bedside lamp offered. His eyes had just adjusted when Tamara flicked the overhead lights on.

She let out a relieved sigh. "It's not pretty, but at least it looks clean."

That about summed it up. He dropped his duffle on the turquoise and yellow bedspread and turned around to face her. "So let's have it."

He'd spent his life surrounded by women. He'd learned the hard way that ignoring the elephant in the room only made them more pissed off. He should have filled her in during the drive, but he didn't. He was an asshole. So what?

So you made a shitty situation worse, Camacho.

She dropped her bag on the small table by the window and strutted forward until she was inches away from him. Her anger vibrated off of her, pressing against his skin and setting every nerve ending on edge—not because he worried she'd strike out, but because he loved it when she lost her icy reserve. He really was a bastard—a horny one with a hard-on for bitchy blondes.

"When were you going to fill me in on the plan to have Marko and Elisa spend the night at the compound?" She jabbed her finger into his chest. Hard. "When are we going in?" Another jab as heat rose in her cheeks. "When are we getting Essie?"

He wrapped his fingers around her hand and tugged it down to the side. He could have let go of her. He should have let go of her, but he didn't. The sparks of awareness zipping up his arm before diving lower felt too good to let go.

"Marko and Elisa didn't have a choice," he said, trying his hardest to focus on the mission and not the woman driving him nuts. "The only way to get on the compound on short notice was to say they were passing through on a planned vacation. Fane's people offered to let them stay the night. Their cover story is that they are considering joining the Society and bringing a shit ton of cash with them. They had to say yes."

"The longer Essie is there, the greater the chance Jarrod is going to sell her off to one of his followers." She took in a shaky breath. "We have to get there before it's too late."

Damn. He hated that little hitch in her voice because he knew just how much it cost her. If there was anyone in the world who hated being vulnerable or needing help, it was Tamara Post. He wanted to pull her close, wrap his arms around her like he had at Albert's house, and reassure her that everything was going to be okay. But that wasn't the way things worked between them anymore. She'd made her wishes clear.

"We will." He let go of her and took a step back. He needed space, breathing room. The woman was making his thinking muddy. "The plan is for Marko and Elisa to get a full look at the compound. We need to know where everything is situated before we can do the extraction. They'll report back here tomorrow morning. The Feds are flying in tomorrow morning to act as as backup if we need it."

The pink in her cheeks turned to red. "What about me?"

He was ready for this one. "You'll stay here. You're not an operative."

She opened her mouth to argue, no doubt, but closed it without a word. Isaac mentally marked it on his calendar. It wasn't every day that Tamara didn't have a lightning-fast comeback to something.

Finally, she harrumphed and paced a path on the worn carpet going between the door and the king-sized bed. "Waiting around until tomorrow doesn't seem right. She's my niece. I promised to protect her."

It would bust his chops if he was the one not going, too. He couldn't blame her for being frustrated, but nothing was going to change this.

"It's the way it's got to be done." He clasped his hands behind his back before he lost the battle to touch her again. She'd made the call to end things between them. He wasn't so hard up that he had to chase after women who had no interest in getting caught. "We go in blind and there's a chance we won't get Essie out of there at all. Fane is armed and his people are fanatical. That's a shitastic combination. We have to do this right."

She stopped pacing and stood with her arms crossed and one hip popped out, all attitude and sass. "So what, I just sit here and twiddle my thumbs all night like a good girl instead of making sure Essie is safe?"

Oh God. The ideas that popped into his head at the mention of all night were very R-rated and totally unobtainable. She'd made the call. There wasn't going to be anything between them. Fine. He just had to think of it as a mission. He had to babysit the client. What would he do with any other client in this situation? There wasn't a TV in the room. He spotted a box of cards in the middle of the small table.

"I was thinking we'd play cards."

As long as it wasn't strip poker, he just might survive the night without losing his mind.

CHAPTER TWENTY

Elisa

Being someone else could be fun—like trying on an expensive pair of leather pants and knowing you'd never buy them, but still loving the way they made your ass look. Other times, it was exhausting, as if you were trudging your way through a muddy swamp in high heels. Pretending to be a gun-toting, hate-filled, prospective cult member sure as hell fell into the second category.

Elisa shut the heavy oak door behind her and managed to keep her game face on, pretending to admire all of the homey touches to the guest cottage while Marko swept the place for bugs of the video and audio variety using what looked like a cell phone. The member of the Crest Society were paranoid sons of bitches, and she wouldn't put it past them to have the cottage on a closed-circuit video and audio feed. It's exactly what she would have done.

"We're good." He pocketed the frequency counter and sat down on the corner of the bed. "Next time I say I'm up for a little undercover, please remind me of today."

Like he ever listened to her about anything. If he did, she would have already seen all those glorious muscles of his up close and personal. The B-Squad was full of prime hotness, but no one was quite like Marko. He was big—six feet five inches big—and built like a tank covered in tattoos. He had dark eyes, black hair, a trim beard, and steel bars that ran through his nipples. The last bit she'd spotted when he'd swapped shirts on a mission a few months ago. To her utter disappointment, that was all the clothing he'd taken off. Good thing she had an amazing imagination to fill in all the blank spots—one that was already putting images in her head that involved lots and lots of exposed, tattooed skin and hard muscle.

"What? You didn't have fun in Patriarchy Land?" she asked, teasing him to get herself back on level ground before she lost focus, a definite problem around him.

"Not even close." He let out a long sigh and pinched the bridge of his nose. "Plus I never set eyes on Fane."

"He must be keeping a close watch on Essie." She stopped in front of Marko, standing between his parted legs, and turned around. "Unzip me so I can get out of this thing."

The tight collar on the sister wives' horror of a dress had scratched against her neck all day. The only thing that sounded better than busting Marko's chops was getting the stupid outfit off.

"Can't you do it yourself?"

Dudes. They did not understand the pain of being a girl. "Asks the man who's never been trapped in a dress that's half on and half off. Help."

There was a moment of utter stillness behind her before strong fingers grasped the zipper and lowered it down to her ass in a rush. The back of her dress flapped open and she took a deep breath of freedom.

"Thank God. I thought that thing was going to choke me." She shimmied out of the dress and stepped over the pile of material at her feet while luxuriating in the cool air-conditioned air blowing against her overheated skin. "Women's retreat." She barked out a hard laugh and rolled her sore shoulders. "More like detention center. I spent the day sweating my ass off making bread in a hot kitchen while you had your little tour. Please tell me you learned something worthwhile."

"Get dressed," he said, his deep voice strained. "Then we'll talk."

She went still. Claustrophobia had been clawing away at her all day thanks to that dress, and she hadn't been able to think past the relief of getting the damned thing off. Now that her fear of being constrained wasn't shredding her control, she looked down.

Oops.

She was wearing a black bra and boy shorts the Crest Society would definitely not approve of and a pair of nondescript ballet flats. The undergarments covered more than her string bikini but, judging by his tone, not enough for Marko. Her smirk came automatically. She couldn't help it. Something about teasing the quiet giant just plain did it for her. Oh, this was going to be fun.

· Elisa managed to smother her grin before putting a hand on one hip and turning around to face him. "What's wrong?"

He stared at a spot right over her right shoulder, tension squaring his jaw. "You're in your underwear."

She cocked her head, playing the dumb routine to the hilt. "Uh-huh?"

Marko's dark gaze slid over her, blasting heat across every millimeter of bare skin. "Cut the crap, Elisa."

Poking the bear was a bad idea, but damn, it sure was fun. She glanced down at herself and then back up at Marko, taking enough time to enjoy the view from his thick thighs to his broad chest to his glowering face. This was their game. She teased. He resisted. They both knew eventually it would come to a head. She just hoped her headboard would survive the encounter.

Fuck that. She'd be disappointed if it did.

"It's more than I wear to the beach, but I don't want to make you uncomfortable."

"Yeah, you do."

She gave him the big-eyed look that always made men stupid. "Why would I want that?"

"It helps you distance yourself."

Bam. His words hit like a solid punch to the head, just enough to shock you silent but not enough to knock you out. She took a protective step back and was lifting her foot to take another before she caught herself and flipped him the bird.

"Whatever." She strutted over to her suitcase, which some Crest Society flunky had brought from the truck, and unzipped it before pulling out an oversized T-shirt and putting it on. It hung down to mid-thigh. "Better?"

He uncurled the fists he'd held tight to his thighs, but otherwise didn't acknowledge her question. "There are armed patrols on the perimeter and surveillance cameras at regular intervals. Once inside, only the guards are armed, and they're stretched thin because so many men are working outside the compound."

That wasn't how the Crest Society had worked in Daddy Fane's day. Back then they were a self-supporting operation. Looked like junior wasn't up for the task. At least not without an influx of money.

"That explains why he's so anxious for Mark Ryan's cash."

Marko nodded. "Exactly."

The information was good, but not the kind Clay Blackfish's friends at the ATF were looking for. They cared about weapons, not problematic change management.

"Did you spot anything that will get the Feds all hot and bothered?" she asked.

His mouth curled into an ornery grin. "Just the armory. Lots of stuff in there that Uncle Sam does not clear for sale to the general public."

"So why'd they show it to you?"

"Because I'm just that damn charming." Marko practically snarled his response, obviously not liking anyone questioning his abilities.

She lifted an eyebrow, but let it go. Marko was many things—intimidating, smart, tough, sexy as hell—but a sweet talker he was not. "Don't tell Lash. He'll think he's out of a job."

Marko snorted. "What did you find out?"

"I was with all the women, remember?" she asked in her best Southern belle accent while batting her lashes. "What could they possibly know?"

He didn't say anything. He didn't have to. The don't-bullshit-me look on his face was enough.

"Fine." She shrugged. "Fane is having problems. We already knew about the money, but he's losing his power base. Too many of the patriarchy patrol saw him agreeing to a divorce as bad enough. That he let Tamara steal away with Essie was about as bad as it could get. There's talk of getting a new leader. Some think you and I are here to be Fane's replacement."

That last bit was what had made the ladies so chatty. When you depended on others for so much of your survival, you learned to always keep your options open during a power play.

"So why would Fane welcome us with open arms?"

"Maybe he didn't have a choice." She paced in front of the bed, rolling the problem in her head like a multi-colored marble that looked different depending on how the light shone through it. Finally it hit her. "To not let us in would be as good as admitting weakness."

"More than a pretty face, aren't you?"

She executed a quick bow that brought her face level with his chest and the faint outline of those tempting bars against his T-shirt. Desire rolled through her, hot and hungry, as she straightened.

"Care to find out? Does the submissive miss get you going?" She lowered her gaze to the floor. "I can put the dress back on." She grasped the edge of her T-shirt and inched it up higher. "Or maybe it's the opposite and you're looking for a dirty girl to do all sorts of naughty things." She met his gaze, saw the same lust burning her up inside in his dark eyes. "Come on, Marko. I know the thought of it turns you on. Tell me what you want."

He stood up slowly, and the full impact of him hit her hard. It was more than just his size or the steely control he seemed to exert just by breathing. It was all of him. The testosterone-filled manliness of him. It sounded dumb even in her head, but there was just no other way to describe it. He was strong, self-contained, and devastatingly male. It took her breath away.

"You." He reached up and glided his thumb across her bottom lip. "No act, no fake personality. I want Elisa Sharp."

The declaration was a sudden wind that blew out a candle flame. All the heat, the wonder, the lust disappeared. No one got her. No one got the real Elisa. She'd made sure of that.

"You couldn't handle me." It sounded defensive even to her own ears.

"More like you can't handle you," he said, all the gruffness in his voice replaced with a softness she didn't understand and sure as hell didn't want.

This wasn't how this was supposed to go. Then again, it never was with Marko. He was the one man who didn't fall prey to her con. Time for her to smarten up and cut her losses. She jutted out her chin and blew him a kiss.

"I'll leave you to your little therapy session then." She whirled around.

"I'm taking a shower."

Years of practicing how to present just the right facade got her across the room and into the bathroom, where she could get her brain straight under pounding hot water before she admitted out loud just how on the money he'd been.

CHAPTER TWENTY-ONE

Tamara

Not even the royal straight in Tamara's hand or the 300- point lead she had in rummy softened the hard grip of anxiety threatening to choke her. A golden glow from the lights in the motel's parking lot seeped in around the edges of the closed curtains. Wrappers from her vending machine dinner filled the trash can by the door. The third can of soda hadn't been a good idea for her nerves—not that anything short of having Essie back was going to do a damn thing to help.

"This is ridiculous." She tossed her cards face-down on the table.

"Your hand?" Isaac asked, keeping his own cards in his hand and his voice carefully neutral.

"No, sitting here playing cards while God-knows-what is going on at that compound." She shoved her chair back and stood up.

The need to move wasn't just optional, it was almost beyond her control. Frustration, worry, the lack of control, it all whirled around inside her, forming a tighter knot with every step she paced in the narrow space between the table and the bed.

Isaac laid his cards on the table, slow and steady. "We've been over this."

That tone. She knew that tone. It was the bitches-be-crazy-so-talk-calmly tone. Maybe she was crazy. In this moment, she didn't give a fuck. Essie was in danger and Tamara was stuck sitting in a motel room miles away, being told to sit and wait like a pretty little girl should. She'd promised Amelia—promised her—that she'd keep Essie safe.

"I know. Of course I know," she seethed, the anger rushing through her like a fast-moving wave of lava. "I'm just a calculating opportunist. If you're looking for a sugar daddy then I'm your girl, but when it comes to doing anything important I am just another empty-headed blonde." She was yelling and she couldn't stop herself. The volume, the words, the emotion, they were out of her control. "Just look at the mess I've made of everything so far."

"What in the hell are you talking about?" he snapped back, tension stringing his shoulders tight. "Would it have been better if you'd just left Essie with her dad?"

"Hell no." That hadn't even been an option, not for a single second.

"You can't control everything, no matter how hard you try. Haven't you realized that by now?"

"I learned that a long time ago." She continued to pace as the memories came at her one after the other, making her scared that she'd drown in the bitter real-life nightmares of how she'd grown up. "My mother made sure I knew exactly what my limitations were."

Isaac got up and walked into her path. He stood there, a mountain she couldn't move. He didn't reach out. He didn't take her by the shoulders and shake her. He was just there like a constant on a map—exactly what she needed, wanted, craved. The realization jerked her to a stop and made her already racing pulse go into hyper-drive.

"She sounds like mom of the year material."

"You have no idea." The heat had seeped out of her, replaced by an almost eerie calm, an emptiness waiting to be filled. "By the time I was fourteen, I was in training—not for a pageant, but for landing a rich man. By sixteen, I had one of my own. By eighteen, I had several. Do you want to know how many men I've slept with because they were rich and looking for something pretty to hang on their arm? Too many. I was a rich man's trophy for too long to not know exactly what my limitations are."

This was why she built that cool reserve around her like castle walls, because once it started to fall, anyone could see all her vulnerabilities. That was the real lesson her mom had taught her—never let them see you weaknesses. Her mother had known Tamara's, and she'd exploited every one.

Isaac reached out, but Tamara swerved around him and resumed her pacing. If he touched her now, she'd fall apart. She wouldn't—couldn't—let that happen.

"You're more than that," he said, pivoting to face her even as she walked away. "It's time you stopped letting you mom's twisted opinion of you be your own."

Her step faltered and her head snapped up. The truth of his words slammed into her, shaking the fragile grip she had on her emotions. The moment the first angry tear slid down her cheek, she vowed to make him pay, make him hurt as much as she did. She spun around, hands on her hip and glared at him as he stood there all self-righteous. Too bad for him she knew right where to hit.

"Says the man who can't bring himself to admit that he's so desperate for a place to belong—a tribe of his own—that he hangs on the edges of his family and of the B-Squad just to get a glimpse of what he won't let himself have."

He started, his eyes darkening with fury. "Fuck you."

"Why, because I'm right?" She hurled the question back at him.

"You don't know what the hell you're talking about."

But she did. She was sure of it. If there was one thing she excelled at besides makeup and a spectacular baton-twirling routine, it was knowing what men wanted—what they really wanted. She'd spent her life studying them, understanding them, anticipating their desires. Looking at Isaac as he watched her, horror and anger flitting across his face, she knew she was right. And she wished like hell she wasn't, because it meant he'd spent years hurting himself the worst way he could.

"Sure I do, and deep down you know it," she said, all her rage gone. She walked back to him. "The first time we met, you told me you don't play well with others. That was a lie. You are the consummate team player and you can't help but be the hero people need, but you're too busy punishing yourself for what happened in Afghanistan to let yourself be the man you're meant to be."

"Shut up," he said, barely getting the two words out through his clenched jaw.

"Why?" She gave him a small smile, the kind that promised it would be okay. "Because the bitchy blonde is right?"

He didn't say anything. He just stood there, his entire body locked tight while he stared at something over her shoulder. Then, slowly, his muscles relaxed and his gaze slid over to her.

"Yes." One corner of his mouth tilted up. "The bitchy blonde is right."

Relief flooded through her and the breath she'd been holding whooshed out just in time for guilt to sneak in and take up residence. "I'm sorry. I shouldn't have said all that. It wasn't my place"

He shrugged those broad shoulders of his. "It's about time someone did, because you're right. And that just goes to prove that you're a helluva lot more than what your mother drilled into your head."

It was pretty to think so but... "I'm scared."

"Of what?"

She took a deep breath. If she didn't do it now, she wasn't sure she ever would.

"I'm scared that she's right. I failed with Amelia, letting her disappear into Jarrod's world without a fight. I failed Essie because I let him get to her. Failed the B-Squad because they're out there risking their lives for the office secretary."

"That's bullshit." He snorted. "You didn't fail. Amelia asked you to save her daughter, and that is exactly what you're doing. We're getting her back and we're going to help the Feds nail Fane to the wall so he can't ever steal her back again."

It sounded so good when he said it like that. It made her want to believe. "I'm not good at accepting help."

"No shit." He laughed. "But no man—or woman—can do everything on their own. We all need a team."

"Even you?" Sure it was a nudge, but he needed it. She wasn't the only one who'd been spitting in the wind and paying the price.

"Yeah, even me." He closed the distance between them and rested his hand on the upper swell of her hip. "But right now, all I need is you."

"Why?" It was probably the worst question in the world to ask, but she couldn't stop herself.

"I have a thing for bitchy blondes." He dipped his head, letting his lips hover over hers. "Didn't anyone tell you?"

Her heart banged against her ribs and a thin ribbon of fear wound its way through the excitement bubbling up inside her. Falling for Isaac was a risk—the biggest one she'd ever taken. It's why she'd pushed him away and run every time he chased. He wasn't like the others. He was a forever kind of guy. "What if I'm not as bitchy as I pretend to be?"

"I guess I'll just have to learn to live with it." He stayed there, his mouth only a hair's breadth from hers, all but daring her to make the first move.

If there was a decision to make, her heart had already done it, so it was time for her body to catch up. She raised herself up onto her tiptoes and captured his mouth, her tongue demanding entrance, and all the fear, uncertainty of the past few months washed away with the touch.

Her hands snaked around him, sneaking underneath his soft cotton T-shirt, the only thing blocking her from the skin-to-skin contact she craved. She wanted—needed—to touch and taste his warm skin. She yanked the shirt from his jeans, exposing a slim line of bare skin above his low-slung jeans. Electricity sparked between them, traveling from her fingertips to her clit in a bolt of passion. Weaving her hand between the cotton and his skin, she pushed his shirt higher, but not enough.

Isaac broke the kiss, nudging her back far enough to be able to whip off his shirt. "Take your clothes off."

"Is that an order?" She toyed with the hem of her T-shirt, anticipation making her tremble just enough to send her pulse skyrocketing.

Desire flared in his eyes. "Yes."

Cocky and confident, he sat down in the straight-backed chair, ready to enjoy the show. Well if that's what he wanted, she could more than deliver.

"Whatever you say, sir." She released the loose-fitting T-shirt and dropped her hands to the top button of her jeans and flipped it open before inching the zipper down.

Shimmying out of the jeans, she watched Isaac as the battle between his need to touch her and his wanting to watch played out on his face. His hands were gripping the arms of the chair, but he hadn't given in to the urge that she could feel it beating against her skin. It sent a fresh wave of want surging through her, and drawing out the moment didn't seem as fun anymore. She yanked the T-shirt over her head, tossed it onto the bed, and stood before him in only her hot pink lace bra and panties.

Isaac let out a strangled groan and surged out of the chair. He was beside her in two long strides, all heat and hunger and wanting focused totally on her.

"You're taking too long." His voice was strained.

"I thought you were enjoying the show." She looked up into his eyes as she traced a finger around his hard, flat nipple before dipping down to lap at it.

He shivered under her touch and she grazed her teeth over him and lowered her hands over his bare chest, following the dusting of his hair as it narrowed over the hard lines of his abs and disappeared beneath the waistband of his jeans. She brushed her fingertips over the button and opened his jeans. She had his zipper halfway down when he wrapped his strong hands around her wrists and yanked her away from her goal.

"That wasn't nice," she teased, her voice breathy and soft.

Even now, as he had a viselike grip around her wrists, she leaned in toward him, needing to touch, lick, and taste every inch of his warm skin. He tugged her arms higher, pulling her close and drawing her attention from the magnificence of his muscular chest. His face was set in hard lines, his eyes nearly black with lust. Using his free hand, he glided a fingertip over the lace band crossing over her hip, slipping it under the material—far enough to taunt but not enough to please—and eliciting a moan from her.

"You're still wearing too many clothes."

God, she couldn't agree more. "You don't like seeing me in nothing but lace?"

"I will always like that, but tonight I need to feel you." He skimmed the back of his hand up her stomach, setting off jolts of pleasure that ricocheted through her. "I'm going to touch you everywhere, tease those pink nipples of yours until they're so hard and feel so good that you're not sure if it's pleasure or pain, but you're going to beg me not to stop." He cupped one breast, circling his thumb over the lace-covered nipple. "I'll watch you come, and then I'm going to sink deep inside you and make you come again all over my cock."

"That's a big order." She arched her back, pushing more of herself against him, desperate for the little bit of friction.

He rolled her nipple. "And you're already wet just imagining it."

"Cocky bastard."

"When it comes to how fucking unbelievable it can be between us?" He grinned down at her. "You damn right I am."

"Then you'd better let me go so I can take it all off."

No strip tease this time. Tamara wanted her clothes gone and gone fast. The last bit of lace had no sooner than hit the floor when Isaac wrapped an arm around her waist and tossed her onto the bed. Pillows bounced, but she stayed put thanks to the six-feet, four-inch wall of sinewy muscle holding her in place. Propped up on his hands, he was almost in pushup position above her, wearing only his jeans and a devious smile. It was the kind of look that had her biting down on her bottom lip to keep from moaning out loud.

"It's not fair." She reached for his pants. "You still have your jeans on."

"If you're still cognizant enough to talk then I'm not doing my job." He sucked her nipple into his mouth, tugging hard on the sensitive nub.

The smart ass remark she was about to say died on her lips as pleasure verging on blissful pain shot through her. Suddenly his hands and mouth were everywhere. The inward bend of her waist. The round top of her hip. The hollow of her throat. The delicate flesh of her breasts. The sensitive curve of her inner thigh. It was torture. It was heaven. It was all Isaac and she couldn't get enough.

He licked and nibbled his way from one breast to the other as she writhed underneath him. "You taste so sweet."

She wrapped her legs around his waist and arched her back so she could rub herself against him. She was so wet, so desperate for him that the feel of denim against her soft folds was almost enough. "Isaac, please."

"What is it, darlin'?" He nipped at the spot where her neck met her shoulder, unleashing a delicious tingle of sensation across her skin. "What do you want?"

"You." It wasn't just a plea, it was straight-up begging and she didn't care.

He went lower, lazing drawing circles around her nipple with his tongue. "Not yet. You have to let go first."

It was the last thing she wanted to do, but she trusted him in this…and in everything.

Before she could process the realization, he reached between their bodies and sank a single finger between her wet folds. Her back arched in reaction to his touch, so pleasurable it nearly broke her. Eyes clenched shut, neon ribbons danced across her mind's eye, their hues becoming more vibrant as he stroked her clit and dipped first one, then two, then three fingers inside her.

Trying to anchor herself to reality, she reached for him. Her fingers dug into his broad shoulders, but instead of bringing her back to the real world, the feel of his skin increased her need. It pushed her forward and brightened the colors behind her eyelids until they were nearly electric. The vibration built deep inside her, ratcheting up with each stroke of his fingers, in and out. His fingers twisted within her, pushing her closer to release until the colors exploded and her orgasm overtook her.

Isaac

Watching Tamara come down from an orgasm was almost as good as seeing her have one. Her entire body relaxed back onto the bed. Her eyelids had fluttered shut and a small smile played across her lips. Sated and in that weird place between totally conscious and blissed out of her mind, she wasn't just beautiful. She was breathtaking.

She cracked her eyes open. "Why are you looking at me like that? It's the hair, isn't it?"

"No." Still leaning over her, he swept one of the light brown strands away from her face, and he felt like he was seeing her for the first time. "It's like I'm finally getting to see you, not the ice princess."

Tamara let her hands drift across his chest, following the lines of his body like she was trying to memorize it. "I've been here all along."

"I know." And he did Deep down in a place he didn't ever think about or consider, he'd known.

Ever since he'd been exiled from the Marines, part of him had been searching for something to fill that hole—she hadn't been wrong when she'd called him out on that. With Tamara, there was a connection, a sense of belonging that was far stronger than any other he'd ever experienced. If he didn't know better, he'd think it was love.

"I'm not sure I like that look."

"What look is that?" he asked, leaning down to nibble along her neck. A little distraction never hurt.

"The one that says you're thinking too hard when you should be doing other things." She smacked his ass, still covered by his jeans. "Get these off and come show me that the other night wasn't just a fluke, cowboy."

He stood up, planting himself between her splayed legs, and tipped an imaginary cowboy hat. "Yes, ma'am."

He grabbed his wallet from his back pocket. After taking out a condom, he tossed the wallet onto the table next to where her bra had landed and shucked off his jeans. She was all sensual moves and tempting curves as she stood up and took the condom out of his hand.

"Here. Let me." She ripped open the foil package.

Arguing wasn't on his agenda. So he closed his eyes and recalled football stats as she gripped his cock in her cool hand, giving him a few leisurely strokes, before rolling the condom on. Even that small touch from her was enough to make his balls tingle.

"You promised me a turn on the table."

He glanced back at the little table littered with cards, her bra and his wallet. It had wobbled while they'd been playing cards. Fucking on it might mean the end of the thing. "Next time." He sat down on the bed and curled a finger at her. "Come here."

She did so without argument, swaying her hips with ever step. It was a sight he wouldn't ever get tired of seeing.

"You're beautiful."

"You ain't so bad yourself." She pushed a finger against his shoulder, pushing him so he was flat on his back on the bed. "Now behave yourself and I'll show you how much fun I can be."

He couldn't fucking wait.

She got on the bed, straddling him, and lowered herself down onto his cock, taking him as deep as he could go. He had half a breath to enjoy her tight hold before she rotated her hips and rode his cock like they'd both been made for this, for each other. She pressed her palms against his chest and her arms framed her generous tits. The temptation to touch was one he wasn't about to deny.

Reading up, he took her nipples between his finger and thumb and rolled the hard flesh, eliciting a low moan from her parted lips. Wanting to hear that sweet sound again, he tugged them gently and curled upward so he could circle one pink nipple with his tongue before sucking it into his mouth.

"Oh God, yes," she cried out, leaning back and pressing her hips into him.

The move allowed him to sit all the way up. He slid his hands around to her back to help her maintain her balance as she continued to ride him, picking up her pace and doing a figure eight thing with her hips that made his balls tighten. God, he was close. He wanted her there with him.

He pulled her close, angling his hips so that her clit hit his pubic bone with each downward stroke.

"Fuck yes," they called out together.

She ground her wet folds against him, clinging to him, massaging his cock with every stroke until he was on the edge of coming. He grabbed her full hips with the intention of slowing her down and making it last, but instinct took over. He lifted his hips and pulled her down hard on his cock again and again as she undulated, rubbing herself against him.

He couldn't wait. He already had played on the edge for too long. Already his balls were tight, ready to spill.

The slap of their bodies meeting filled his ears and a musky scent surrounded them. Her body, so warm and smooth underneath his palms, pushed him to go faster but he wanted to draw it out a little bit longer, just a little bit longer. He could make it last. Hold her longer. Bring her closer. Make her his. But then her body stiffened and her wetness squeezed his cock as she came. Her orgasm milked his cock and he gave in. His climax hit him and everything went black. He held onto Tamara like she was the only thing in the world that mattered.

They collapsed together on the bed. Too tired to do more than wrap her up in his arms and brush a kiss across her forehead, he did just that before drifting off in the way that only a man who'd found his home could.

CHAPTER TWENTY-TWO

Tamara

The arm around Tamara's waist tightened, pulling her closer to the warm, long line of Isaac's body as she tried to orient herself in the dark room. The first rays of dawn were peeking through the blinds. It wasn't bright enough to wake her up...but something had. There wasn't any movement in the room beyond the rhythmic rise and fall of Isaac's chest and his deep, steady breaths were the only sound.

Nerves? Anxiety? Stress? Probably all of the above.

It'll all work out. It has to. She repeated the mantra and relaxed back into Isaac's arms, the springy curls of his chest hair tickling her back.

That's when she heard it. The soft buzz of her phone vibrating. Heart hammering against her ribs, she jackknifed into a sitting position. Completely awake and utterly terrified, she grabbed the cell off the bedside table. Only one person would be calling the burner phone.

"Essie," she answered. "Are you okay?"

"Oh she's fine," a man said.

A cold shiver worked its way up her spine. "Jarrod, you bastard. How you get this number?"

"You've given my little girl some very devious ideas." He didn't sound happy about it. "She actually managed to hide her phone up until now. One of the ladies helping her get ready for her big day found it and handed it right over to me."

Isaac sat up next to her, scooting in close. She tilted the phone out far enough for him to lean in and hear both sides of the conversation.

"Let Essie go," she said, fighting to keep her voice as neutral as possible.

"Don't worry, I will. First thing tomorrow afternoon after the minister pronounces them man and wife. She'll be on her way out of the country right after the ceremony."

Fear shoved her stomach down to her toes. "You can't."

"I surely can. You two have caused me quite a bit of trouble. My followers expect a show of strength."

And the bastard would give it to them. It didn't matter what happened to Essie. For Jarrod, it was all about doing whatever it took to maintain his control over the Crest Society. It always had been. He could have his little cult. She just wanted Essie safe. There was bargaining to be done or else he wouldn't have made the call.

She glanced over at Isaac. He was still naked, his hair was going every which way and a shadow of dark stubble on his jaw, but he was the picture of focus. She could practically see him memorizing every syllable Jarrod said. No doubt a plan was already starting to form in Isaac's head. She just had to do her part—and she would.

"What do you want, Jarrod?" she asked.

"You. Here. "

"I'm in Texas."

He laughed. It wasn't a nice sound. "Don't lie to me. Bryson, your waiter at the diner, told me you only wanted coffee. The brown hair was a nice touch, but you never were skilled enough to pull of any kind of role beyond that of gold-digging beauty queen."

"Why wait until now to reach out?" Her pulse sped up in alarm and her palms became clammy, making her adjust her hold on the phone. Did he know about Marko and Elisa? Where they in danger now, too? "You know I've been here since yesterday."

"This might come as a shock to you, but you are not the center of the universe. Anyway, I have nothing to fear from you and your latest idiot boyfriend," Jarrod said, the confidence in his tone bordering on self-delusion. "Now get your ass up, ditch your latest sugar daddy loser and get over here. I want my followers to come to breakfast this morning and see you sitting by my side. You will confess your wrongdoing. You will beg for mercy."

"I suppose you'll be in a generous mood." Like he even had a clue what that meant.

"Always. In fact, I'll announce that I'm so glad to have my daughter back in the fold that I just can't bear to let her go just yet. The bridegroom will be disappointed, I'm sure, but he'll have no choice but to accept it."

She glanced over at Isaac, the calm look in his eyes settling her and making it easier to think. Jarrod hadn't mentioned Marko or Elisa. If he'd known they were in on the rescue mission, he would have used them for extra leverage. That meant they'd still be able to get Essie out of there this afternoon as planned. All she had to do was let Jarrod think he had all the power. The megalomaniacal jerk already thought he did so it wouldn't take much convincing. She just couldn't give in too easily.

"And if I say no?" she asked.

"You don't want to say no. I know Essie's hoping you won't. Her groom will be thrilled though, he can't wait to take her home...wherever in the world that may be. You know, he was really hoping for a morning wedding. I told him no, but I could change my mind."

She couldn't let Essie get taken out of the country. "Fine. I'll come"

"One of my followers will pick you up in front of the diner in five minutes," Jarrod said. "Be ready."

The phone went dead.

She bounded out of the bed, grabbing her clothes from the floor and pulling them on—a real trick when her hands were shaking as badly as they were.

Isaac grabbed her arm as she was pulling up her jeans. "You can't be serious about going. There's got to be another way."

God, she wished there was. Dread sat like a chunk of concrete in her stomach. There would be more coming her way when she stepped inside the compound. She knew it. Isaac knew it. Whatever Jarrod had planned for her would be, at the very least, a lesson in public humiliation.

"We don't have a choice." She shook his hand off and yanked up her jeans. "Anyway it's just a delay until Marko and Elisa get back and you three make your move. I wasn't part of that plan, remember. This changes nothing, but if it keeps Jarrod from forcing Essie down the aisle before you guys can get there, then I have to do it."

Isaac stood up and tugged her T-shirt out of her hands before she could put it on, anger making his body rigid. "You have no idea what he's really up to. It's a trap."

She peeked around the corner of the window blinds. Across the gravel parking lot, a dust-covered sedan sat idling in front of the diner. Turning back, she drank in the sight of Isaac. He looked like a naked avenging angel, all righteous fury and determination.

"It doesn't matter what Jarrod's up to." A calmness slid through her at the sight of him. "I trust you. I know you'll come for me."

And she did. As surely as baton twirling would always get mocked as the most useless of beauty queen talents, Isaac would always be there for her. Just like she would be for him. That's just how love worked.

She slid the T-shirt from his grasp and slipped it on before raising up on her tiptoes and brushing her lips across his. "I'll see you soon."

He didn't like it, but he didn't stop her when she walked out into the early morning quiet.

Isaac

The sound of gravel crunching under tires was the first good thing to have happened since he stupidly let Tamara walk out of the motel room fifteen minutes ago. He picked up his nine millimeter and went to the window. Part of him was hoping for some of Fane's men. Busting heads sounded really fucking good right about now.

He didn't recognize the truck, but there was no mistaking the couple who got out and headed straight for his room. He hustled across the room and yanked open the door.

Marko had one hand up as if he'd been about to knock. He was wearing jeans, a western-style button-down shirt, and a baseball cap advertising some kind of corn seed. He looked like a good old boy farmer. Elisa looked like she'd just walked off the set for a movie about pioneers.

"Where in the hell have you been?" Isaac asked, standing to the side so they could come in.

Elisa drew her sunglasses down and peeked over the tops at him. "I thought we were smack dab in the middle of crazy town, but it looks like that's actually here."

They strode inside and he closed the door. "Tamara's gone. Fane used Essie's phone to call her. She's on her way there. You probably passed her on the road."

Marko and Elisa jolted to a stop and turned to face him.

"What the glorious fuck," Elisa muttered.

Yeah. That just about summed it up. Half-grateful for having something to do instead of sitting her twiddling his thumbs like an asshole, Isaac hit the highlights and brought them up to speed. By the time he was done, he was jacked up and ready to go in and tear Fane apart, limb from limb.

"We have to go in," he said, fisting his hands. "Now."

Marko and Elisa just looked at each other. He didn't like that look. He knew for sure he wasn't going to like what came out of Marko's mouth when the big man drew himself up and stiffened his shoulders as if he was expecting a blow.

"The Feds will be here in an hour," Marko said. "We can move up the exfil timeline, but not to now."

Fuck 'em. Isaac would take care of it himself. Bianca had called him a lone wolf. Well, maybe it was time he really lived up to the reputation.

"Fine. You wait." The words exploded out of his mouth. "I'll go now."

"You can't do this on your own." Marko's voice was calm but firm. "You need us. You need the team."

Fury rushed like lava through Isaac's veins. He wanted to roar in frustration. Hammer his fists into Jarrod Fane. Take out anyone in his way. He did not want to wait.

"We have to operate under the assumption that it's a trap," Elisa said as she started to pace the small room. "Fane may not realize who we are or who you are, but if he does then he's expecting us. That place has enough firepower to blow us out of the water. Marko's seen it. The Feds totally want in on this. We have to do this smart. We need to give Blackfish's ATF friends a heads up about what to expect on the ground. The last thing we want is for everything to go south and Tamara or Essie to end up getting hurt—or worse."

The idea of a world without Tamara sucked the air out of Isaac's lungs. Goddammit, he did not want them to be right…but they were. He took a deep breath, trying for that yoga calm his mom was always talking about. He failed miserably. The urge to bust open Jarrod Fane's head was too strong for anything else. He'd have to content himself with knowing that he'd get his chance to take the bastard down—soon.

"I'll get Blackfish on the phone." He pulled his cell out of the back pocket of his jeans and scrolled through the contacts. "You two work on diagraming the compound so we can nail down a plan that will get us in and get Tamara and Essie out."

"Listen to you, sounding like a team leader," Elisa said, peeling off the dress to reveal a snug black T-shirt and pants underneath.

"Got a problem with that?" he retorted.

"Negative." Marko shook his head and shot Elisa a dirty look. "Stop busting his chops just because you always get nervous before a mission and need a release."

She flipped him off. "Stop acting like you know everything about me."

"More than you wish I did, sweetheart," Marko said before handing Isaac a list of illegal firearms that he'd spotted in the Crest Society's armory.

The insults and banter were the familiar sound of a team getting ready for battle. He'd heard it a million times before. It was a mix of nerves, adrenaline, and bravado, along with big dose of fuck-yeah-let's-do-this. He'd missed it—needed it—more than he'd ever allowed himself to admit.

Finally, he found the number he was looking for and hit dial.

The DEA agent in Fort Worth answered on the first ring. "Blackfish."

"Hey Clay. We need to get word to the ATF guys. They aren't backup. We have more than enough firsthand information about the Crest Society's armory that says they're going to want to go in with us."

"Talk."

He did and it felt good. They would get Tamara and Essie, and they'd do it as a team.

Tamara

The Crest Society compound was surrounded by a tall chain link fence, the kind usually found around prisons, which seemed fitting. Bryson, the waiter from the diner, turned out to be the driver of the sedan. He'd gone the entire 30 mile drive without saying a word to Tamara. Fine by her. The silence gave her time to get her icy defenses back up.

By the time the guards stopped them at the gate, her back was ramrod straight and her eyes as bored as a teenage girl listening to a lecture from her parents. After a quick look in the car, the guards waved them though. They looked mean with their semiautomatic rifles, but they obviously weren't trained and didn't expect even the tiniest bit of resistance from her or they would have searched her.

It was just the kind of mistake that Isaac and the others would take advantage of when they arrived.

That thought kept her calm as Bryson drove through the compound. He passed four rows of buildings and single-story homes lined up one in front of the other and headed to a two story log cabin next door to a rustic chapel. Another set of armed guards were stationed outside the cabin's front door.

Both men were built like brick houses, but only one came down the steps. He opened up her door, watching her with the cold empty stare of professional muscle. She stepped out, but the guard blocked her path.

"Turn around," he said.

She did and he patted her down like he'd been trained to do it. Vivi had started to teach her some of the basics and Tamara recognized the technique. Looked like Jarrod kept his paid muscle closest to him. The man was a crazy jackass, but he wasn't dumb.

The guard stepped back. "You can go in now."

Even though her stomach was doing that fluttery thing that it always used to before she went on stage, she kept her movements smooth as she strode up the three steps to the porch. The other guard knocked on the front door.

"Send her in," came the muffled reply.

The guard opened the door, revealing a small, empty foyer. The smell of bacon, cigars, and musty books wafted out. It wasn't overwhelming, but it was more than enough to make her already nervous stomach do a quick flip-flop. For half a second, she was frozen to the spot outside the door. But then an image of Essie in a wedding dress flashed in her mind, and then Tamara was walking—strutting—into Jarrod's house with one of the guards following close behind.

The living room was right off the foyer. Jarrod was in front of a fireplace. Standing tall and confident in his crisp white shirt, dark tie, and conservative haircut, he looked like an accountant or a school board president or some other trusted figure. The guise suited his purpose well and he played it to the hilt, giving her a big smile and reaching out to her for a handshake.

"Well, if it isn't Miss Iceberg Lettuce. Or was it Miss Myron County?" he asked, as if it wasn't a dig at all.

Whatever his game was, she wasn't playing. She tugged her hand free of his two-fisted grip. "It doesn't matter. Where's Essie?"

Some of the shine went out of his blue eyes. "In the next room."

"I want to see her before I say anything to your people."

"Don't worry," he said, a sliver of something dangerous in his innocuous words. "You will."

The guard behind her wrapped his arm like an iron bar across her chest and held her tight enough that she couldn't pull free. He slapped his other hand across her mouth. She bit down on the soft fleshy part of his palm, but it was too late. Jarrod picked up a syringe from the fireplace mantle and shoved it into the vein at the crook of her elbow.

Whatever it was, it hurt as it burned its way through her. She opened her mouth to scream, but suddenly it seemed like doing so would take too much energy. The tension in her body seemed to melt away and a cotton-swab soft fog wrapped itself around her.

"Don't worry," Jarrod said. "It's just a sedative to keep you nice and calm while you get ready for the wedding."

"You promised." The words came out slow and a little slurred.

"Yes. But after receiving a vision, I knew what I had to do." That fanatical gleam came into his eyes, making them sparkle as if he was powered by an other-worldly source. "Having you apologize isn't enough. You have to make up for your transgression. How better to show your remorse than to submit as only a wife of mine can?"

This was bad—very bad. He wouldn't be so happy if it wasn't, but she couldn't wrap her addled brain around it. "What are you talking about?"

"A double wedding, of course. There's no better way to show my strength and the truth of my word than having those who defied me voluntarily repent and pledge their devotion to the true believers."

Panic shot through her. "You crazy bastard."

His hand sailed through the air and his palm connected with her cheek. Pain exploded in her head. If the bodyguard hadn't still been holding her up, she would have ended up on the floor.

"Watch that mouth of yours." Jarrod loomed over her, anger leaving red blotches on his cheeks. "I've been exceedingly tolerant of you up until now. Don't expect it to last. Karen!"

A woman rushed through a door next to the fireplace. She had a white cap on her head and a plain brown dress that covered her from throat to ankle.

"You have two hours to get her ready." Jarrod picked up a second syringe from the fireplace mantle and handed it to the woman. "If she starts getting mouthy, give her another shot."

The woman nodded but kept her eyes downcast.

The guard half pulled/half walked her toward the door. Although fear and pain had helped clear the fog, Tamara kept her face slack. Isaac and the rest of the team would be here in a matter of hours. She had until then to find Essie and prepare her to get the hell out of there. If Jarrod and his goons thought she was woozy, that could only help her cause. She just prayed Jarrod hadn't lied about Essie still being at the compound.

Tamara staggered through the doorway and into the other room with almost all of her attention focused downward. She was only partially faking how hard the drug had hit her. Whatever the fuck Jarrod had used, she sure as hell did not want a second dose.

"Aunt T!"

Tamara's head snapped up and she fought back the instant wave of relief at seeing the one person she'd desperately wanted to find on the compound. "Essie!"

The girl rushed to her side and wrapped her arms around Tamara's waist. Tamara buried her face in Essie's blonde hair and couldn't stop the tears when she smelled the girl's favorite vanilla shampoo. She must have finagled her way into packing a few things before they'd left Hamilton, which explained how she'd managed to sneak her phone onto the compound. Essie's plan hadn't worked, but the girl was definitely a fighter and that would serve her well when the shit hit the fan.

Essie pulled back and Tamara got her first good look at her niece. Her eyes were swollen from crying, but there weren't any bruises or other visible signs of abuse.

"Are you okay?" Tamara asked.

The girl nodded. Her face was clean of makeup and she was wearing a simple white dress, both of which made her look even younger than her sixteen years. The steely determination in her eyes didn't say kid, though. That was the look Amelia had worn when she'd made Tamara promise to keep Essie safe from Jarrod. The man didn't know what he was in for.

Tamara took a quick look around the room. There was a narrow bed against one wall and a trio of women huddled in the corner wearing drab brown dresses with their hair pulled back under white caps. One of the women had tears in her eyes. She gave Tamara a sympathetic nod and dropped the unused syringe into the trash can beside the vanity table. The women might be in the Society, but that didn't mean they were here any more voluntarily than she and Essie were.

"I'm so sorry. This is all my fault," Essie said in a hopeless whisper. "He's making you marry him."

Tamara brushed the girl's hair back and kissed her forehead. "It's not your fault. And I'm not marrying him—and you're not marrying…"

"Phillip." Essie rolled her eyes.

Despite the seriousness of the situation, the typical teenage reaction made Tamara chuckle. "Well, Phillip is out of the picture. We just need to play along for a little while until help arrives."

"How do you know someone's coming?"

Tamara squeezed Essie's shoulders. "Because he'll always be there."

That didn't mean she was going to sit idly by and wait through. The women were there to help Essie and Tamara get ready for their farce of a double wedding, but they may be more helpful in other ways.

CHAPTER TWENTY-THREE

Marko

Marko had just made the turn off the main highway to meet with the ATF agents and go over what they'd found at the compound when his phone buzzed. Squinting against the bright morning sun peeking over the horizon, he glanced down at the phone sitting in the cup holder. The caller ID read "G-girl."

Nosy as always, Elisa leaned over from the passenger seat to get a look at his phone. "You gonna answer that?"

"No." He loved his little sister Gillie, but she was going to have to wait. There were bigger things to deal with than whatever drama she'd managed to stir up today.

"One of your girlfriends?" Elisa asked when the buzzing finally stopped.

"Don't have one." Something she well knew. He'd been going out with his right hand for so long they were practically common law spouses.

She pivoted in her seat and dipped her sunglasses down low over the bridge of her nose. With her hair tied up in a bun and her very conservative, un-Elisa-like shirt buttoned up to her neck, she looked like every dirty librarian fantasy a book nerd ever had.

After giving him a slow up and down, she asked, "Not even one night stands?"

"Nope." Again, information she already knew. It wasn't like they didn't all live in the same building, practically on top of each other and constantly in each other's business. If he'd had an overnight guest, the entire B-Squad would be interrogating her over pancakes the next morning.

Elisa's gaze dropped down to his crotch. "Why not?"

He tightened his grip on the steering wheel and swerved to avoid a pothole in the road leading to the nearby airstrip. "We aren't doing this now."

"Why not?" She pushed her sunglasses back into place, a Cheshire cat grin curling her full red lips upward.

"The mission takes precedence," he said.

"And talking about the reason behind your lack of a sex life is going to distract you from driving across the tarmac to where the ATF's jet is parked?"

"We need to focus." It sounded weak even to his own ears, but it was true. Something about Elisa always seemed to knock his concentration sideways.

"Fine." She shrugged. "Have it your way. I'm sure G-girl will be thrilled to talk with her big stud later."

There was just enough of a thread of bitterness in her voice to get through his thick skull and connect with his brain. No doubt she was picking on him because she was still annoyed he'd called her out last night, but there was more. He was sure of it.

"Jealous?" he asked.

Her body stiffened and her chin went up and inch or three. "No."

Oh, yes she was. Elisa Sharp was jealous. The nice thing to do would be to tell her G-girl was his sister, Gillie. Good thing he'd never been accused of being nice.

"For a con artist, you sure do lie like shit." He stopped the car next to the jet and cut the engine.

"Oh yeah?" She had the door open before he even got the key out of the ignition. "Well for someone with a reputation of being strong and silent, you sure do flap your gums a lot."

She hopped out of the truck and slammed the door behind her before strutting over the where the agents were gathered, while he sat behind the wheel trying to unravel the meaning of this latest development.

CHAPTER TWENTY-FOUR

Isaac

The meet with ATF was at a scenic lookout off the highway, about ten miles away from the Crest Society's compound. The agents had shown up in a convoy of SUVs, black with dark tinted windows that screamed Feds, led by Marko and Elisa in their truck.

A man Isaac didn't recognize got out of the passenger side of the first SUV. He was chomping an unlit cigar and swaggered like he was a massive 'roided-out wrester walking to the ring instead of being five feet, nine inches tall and on the skinny side. Isaac's belly tightened. Shit, they did not have time for the guy to go all Napoleon on him right now.

"Good to meet you, Mr. Hargrove." The man held out his hand. "I understand you have some information you'd like to share with your government."

Isaac snuck a glance at Marko and Elisa standing by their truck as he shook the other man's hand. Elisa rolled her eyes. Marko just shrugged.

"Yes, your friends Mr. and Mrs. Ryan have been very helpful so far." He glanced over at the crude map of the Crest Society's compound Marko had drawn that was sitting on the still-warm hood of Isaac's truck. "That's the ticket. I'm gonna go have a peek while you chat with your friends, Mr. Hargrove."

Isaac stood there, his brain trying to catch up with whatever the fuck was going on while the man strode over to the truck. He was flanked by two ATF agents in black cargo pants and T-shirts who never gave Isaac a single glance.

Marko and Elisa made their way over to Isaac as the other agents got out of the remaining SUVs. There were fifteen men in total, all of whom passed by Isaac, Marko and Elisa as if they weren't even there. They huddled around the man examining the map lying on Isaac's truck.

"Welcome to bizarro land," Elisa said.

"What's the deal?" he asked, frustration bubbling through the confusion. "We don't have time for games."

"Skippy over there"—Elisa jerked his chin toward the man obviously in charge—"wasn't real excited about taking civilians in with him during the raid. The deal is, we keep our cover and hang back until it's time to go in. The ATF's focus is on the guns and securing Fane. Ours is on getting Tamara and Essie out. As far as the Feds are concerned, we're three concerned citizens who provided information on the condition of anonymity, then went back to our safe little civilian homes. It's like they won't even be able to see us on the compound."

"Plausible deniability," Marko said.

The whole thing made his head hurt. "Fuck it. I just want to get in and get Tamara and Essie out. Who the Feds have to justify it to isn't a concern of mine."

He turned around and began heading for the ATF agents, but they broke their huddle before he took more than three steps in their direction. All of them marched to the SUVs, again ignoring his, Marko's, and Elisa's existence. All except for the man in charge. He stopped directly in front of Isaac, wearing a bland smile that didn't reach his eyes.

"Thank you again, Mr. Hargrove for sharing this information with us," the man said. "Too bad it's not really of much help."

He handed the map back to Isaac with a curt nod and walked over to his SUV.

What the fuck? How we're they supposed to coordinate? This was bullshit.

Isaac glanced down at the map. There were several new markings on it —Xs, Os and arrows denoting where agents would be and the general plan of attack. The number twenty was written at the top and circled. By the time he looked back up, the agents were all in their SUVs and beginning to pull back out onto the highway.

He shook his head. They must teach an extra-special class at the ATF about how to be a giant pain in the ass.

"We have twenty minutes until they hit," he said, as Marko and Elisa checked out the map. "While most of the compound's force is dealing with the raid, we'll go in here." He tapped a point on the perimeter parallel to the house Marko had been able to identify as Jarrod's thanks to his earlier tour of the compound. "It's the most logical place to start looking for them."

Marko nodded. "Glad I packed the bolt cutters."

"And here I thought that bag was full of all your favorite shoes," Elisa quipped.

"Let's go," Isaac said. "We've got to be set up and ready to move when the Feds' first flash grenade goes off."

Once that happened the shit would really hit the fan, and he was going to do whatever it took to make sure Tamara and Essie didn't get hurt in the fallout.

Tamara

In the two hours since she'd been drugged, the trio of helper-women had supervised her shower, given her a new, simple white dress to wear, fixed her brown hair in an elaborate braid that wound around her head, and pinned a veil to her head.

Tamara took one last look at herself in the full-length mirror, then let the veil fall into place over her face. She might not look like herself, but she finally felt like herself again. The sedative had worn off enough that her vision had cleared and she didn't have to pluck each thought out of a thick fog of confusion. She'd take the wins where she could get them right now. Inhaling a deep breath, she closed her eyes and calmed her nerves. Isaac and the rest of the team would come. She let the breath out, opened her eyes, and turned to the other women in the room.

Essie kneeled in the middle of the trio of girls, Alison, Janice, and Tiffany. They were young, around Essie's age, and had been assigned as her friends/watchers. All three were married, and Tiffany had the full, round belly of late pregnancy. All three had been runaways who'd thought they'd found a home when they'd arrived at the Crest Society compound. By the time they'd figured out what was involved, it was too late. They were trapped.

A knock on the door made all five women in the bedroom jump.

"It's time," the guard said through the door. "I mean it."

The girls had managed to push off the three earlier attempts by the guard to leave.

"Yes, sir," Alison said as she affixed the white lace veil to the headband woven into Essie's hair. "No more delaying. You have to go."

Essie tried to stand but it was too much for her visibly shaking legs. Alison and Tiffany each took one of her arms and helped her until she was steady.

"I appreciate everything," Essie said like a woman off to the firing squad. "Thank you."

"We wish it could have been more," Janice said, and gave Essie a quick, impromptu hug. "It's best if you just submit right away."

Bile rose in Tamara's throat at the thought of what that submission had meant for Janice, Tiffany, and Alison. They were just girls. Their husbands, they'd informed her, were all in their late forties.

The door swung open. The guard who'd helped Jarrod drug Tamara took up most of the open doorway. A second guard stood right behind him. She and Essie may have been able to scramble away from one guard. Two? That ended that hope.

"I mean it," he said. "Let's go. We need to be there before the guests arrive."

All five of them started forward.

"Not you three." He pointed at the girls. "Just the brides."

The girls squawked in quiet protest, but didn't make a move forward.

Tamara took Essie's hand and whispered, "Don't let the bastards grind you down."

The quote from The Handmaid's Tale seemed to fit perfectly with the situation inside the Crest Society compound. Essie squeezed her hand and they walked through the door, heads high and brave faces firmly affixed under their lacy bridal veils.

Isaac

The bolt cutters snapped through the last of the chain-link fence on the east side of the Crest Society compound. Isaac peeled back the section of fence and held it while Marko and Elisa squeezed through the opening. He followed after.

They moved, silent and quick behind the outer line of cabins, their M4 rifles at the ready. The countdown clock had two minutes on it. They had to get in place before the ATF hit. They had a minute to go by the time they'd made it inside the third ring. Isaac signaled to Marko to cross the dirt alley between the houses to get to the next ring when the flash grenade went off with a loud boom.

After that it was chaos. People screamed. Gunfire sounded.

"Let's go," Isaac hollered, and all three of them took off running.

He cleared the fourth ring of houses and spotted two of Fane's guards rushing two women dressed like brides inside the chapel next to Fane's cabin.

"Let me go!" one of the women hollered.

He couldn't see the bride's face, but there was no mistaking the icy contempt in that order. Tamara was pissed. Good. That meant she was okay. Of course, she'd be better once he got her the hell out of here.

Tamara

Tamara fought with everything she had, but she was not getting out of the guard's grasp. His fingers bit into her wrist, squeezing the small bones together. She cried out in pain. He didn't seem to care. He shoved her through the chapel door and slammed it shut behind her.

The second guard, who'd pulled Essie inside the chapel too, grabbed Tamara by the arm and swung her farther back into the vestibule. She sailed through the air, slamming into the wall. The impact knocked the air out of her and dislodged a short wood staff off the wall. It fell the floor and she followed, sliding down the wall as she fought for breath.

"Stay down and don't fuck with me, and you might make it out of here alive," the guard snarled, turning his attention back to the window.

Essie scrambled over to her and held her hand while Tamara tried to get her air back. Sucking in shallow breaths, she looked around the vestibule. The guard stood to their right, leaning against a sliver of wall off to the side of the window by the front door. An open archway divided the vestibule from the chapel behind them. It was small. Only twenty pews and a podium up on the altar. To their left was a wall with a door. They might be able to make it out while the guard was distracted.

"What's going on?" Essie asked, keeping her voice quiet.

Tamara finally sucked in a full breath. "Isaac's here," she whispered. "And it sounds like he brought friends."

The sound of gunfire went off like firecrackers outside, but it wasn't close. They could get out of here. Hide until Isaac got beyond the outer ring of cabins. She curled her fingers around the staff. It was a little over two feet long, but it was made of hard walnut with the Crest Society logo burned into it. As far as weapons went, it wasn't the greatest, but if the guard got close again she'd be able to whack him over the head with it. Another round of gunfire went off, this time closer. The guard's attention was focused on the activity outside the window. If they were going to make a break for it, they needed to do it now.

Tamara looked over at Essie and held her finger to her lips as she stood, holding the staff behind her back. Essie nodded and followed her lead. Her heart slammed against her rib cage as they shuffle-stepped toward the side door as quietly as possible. Chatter from the guard's walkie-talkie filled the silence, helping to cover the sound of their footsteps. A few more and they'd be at the door. She could almost reach the knob. Another step closer. She reached out and—

"Where do you think you're going?" the guard asked, taking a menacing step toward them.

Tamara didn't think. There wasn't time. She reacted with the only skill she had.

As the big man steamed toward them, she twisted her wrist, increasing her speed on each turn. Finally, she raised her arm and threw the staff at him with all the force she'd used in her pageant days when she'd send a baton skyward, execute a double cartwheel, and then catch it. The staff shot through the air, high and true, cracking him right between the eyes. He crashed to the ground.

Tamara whirled around and reached for the side door, but the front door burst open before she could. Jarrod rushed in, gun drawn.

"You bitch," he yelled, more than a touch of craziness thundering through his words. "You've ruined everything."

Tamara threw herself in front of Essie right as the side door flew open.

Isaac

Isaac rushed through the chapel's side door and time screeched to a halt. The rest of the world fell away until all Isaac could see was Jarrod Fane with his finger on the trigger and the handgun pointed at Tamara's head.

There was no hesitation. No flashback to Afghanistan. No second thought. Isaac fired.

The bullet hit Fane in the shoulder, the power of it knocking him back and sending the gun sailing from his grasp. Tamara kicked the gun out of Fane's reach as Isaac ran across the vestibule, hurdling over the guard, who was out cold.

Relief rushed through Isaac, enough that the adrenaline rush from the rescue seemed puny in comparison. She was safe. His entire body ached with the need to curl around her and confirm it in a way his eyes couldn't, but he knew Tamara was finally safe. Everything from Wolczyk showing up at the engagement party to Essie being kidnapped had led up to him firing his gun at another human being for the first time since Afghanistan. Part of him should be freaking out. But he wasn't. The power of seeing the woman he loved without Fane's threat hanging over her head made it all worth it.

He gathered Tamara in his arms while Marko secured the prisoners and Elisa led Essie into the chapel. It wasn't until that moment that he truly realized how close he'd come to losing her, and it shook him right down to his toes. He didn't know how he was going to convince her to stay in Fort Worth, but he'd figure it out. Now that he'd found her, he wasn't about to let her go.

She pulled back far enough to look up at him. "I knew you'd come."

"Always." He cupped her face and tilted it up. "You can trust me on that."

He leaned down and brushed his lips across hers, needing to say more but knowing now wasn't the time. ATF agents were already streaming into the chapel behind them. He ended the kiss before he was ready.

"Come on. Let's go get Essie."

Tamara nodded, but there was something in her eyes that gave him pause. "One thing first," she said.

She stalked over to where Fane was propped up against a wall with one of the agents squatting in front of him applying pressure to the wound.

"Is he going to be okay?" Tamara asked.

The agent nodded. "A through-and-through."

"Good. I'd hate not to be able to get this in." Her leg shot out, connecting with Fane's balls. "That's for my sister."

Every man in the room winced, but no one said anything as Tamara made her way back over to Isaac. "Let's go get Essie."

Isaac couldn't keep the grin off his face as he tucked her arm into the crook of his and led her into the chapel. Tamara may not be Texas-born, but the girl definitely delivered some Texas justice when needed.

Tamara

From her seat in the back of the ambulance, Tamara had a front row seat when the ATF agents led Jarrod out in cuffs. No doubt they had him on gun charges for all of the illegal firepower in the armory, but she'd get the specifics later. Right now, it was enough to know he wouldn't be bothering Essie ever again. The agents led a patched-up and bruised Jarrod to a transport van already half-full of his handcuffed henchmen, among them the asshole guard who'd helped him shoot her full of sedatives.

"I know the view is good, but I need you to follow the light for me." The paramedic squatting in front of her moved a pen light from left to right, then up and down. "Okay, that looks good. No idea what they injected you with?"

She shook her head. Her vision didn't get fuzzy at all. "All he said was that it was a sedative."

"Any allergies?" the paramedic asked, narrowing his eyes under his bushy gray eyebrows.

"No, and I feel fine." She gave him her best pageant-winning smile.

He harrumphed. "What you should do is go to the hospital for observation just in case, but I don't think you're gonna follow that advice."

She didn't say a thing. Sometimes winning meant keeping your big mouth shut.

The paramedic went on, "Just be careful. If you start feeling dizzy or light-headed at all, come straight to the emergency department." He eyeballed the cut on her cheekbone that had already stopped bleeding.

"Did you really knock the guy out with a baton-twirling trick?"

She nodded, still not quite believing she'd managed to make it happen. Wait until she told Albert.

He laughed as he stood up, clearing her way to leave. "Remind me never to piss off a beauty queen."

"Yeah, we're real brawlers," she said, chuckling. "Thanks for your help."

She got out of the ambulance and began searching for Isaac and Essie. She finally spotted them just past a small group of women and children standing near one of the big black SUVs. An invisible weight lifted off her chest at the sight. Just seeing them was like finding treasure she hadn't known she'd been looking for but was damn glad she'd found.

It took her a minute to get through the swarm of agents, paramedics, and others gathered around the chapel, but she finally made it to their sides. But by the time she got there, they weren't alone anymore. A man with a cold smile and serious eyes in a Kevlar vest with ATF printed across the back in yellow letters was with them.

"Tamara Post?" the man asked.

She nodded.

"You do know there's still a warrant out for your arrest? Transporting a minor across state lines is a federal offense."

Her gut twisted. Instinctively, she reached out for Isaac's hand. Just the touch of his warm fingers helped steady her.

"You don't understand," Essie said, squeezing her body between Tamara's and the agent's. "You guys saw what my father is capable of. She was saving me. If it wasn't for her, he would have—"

The agent held up his hand, stopping Essie mid-rant. "I understand that, but the law is the law."

Isaac stiffened beside Tamara, no doubt ready to pounce on the smaller man, but she squeezed his hand, stopping him before any real trouble could start. That wasn't going to help anything. She'd broken the law. She'd have to pay the price.

"It's all right," she said, swallowing the emotion clogging her throat. "I knew what I was doing when I took Essie."

"And why, exactly, did you do that, ma'am?" the agent asked.

"Because it was the right thing to do." Hell, if she was going to be in handcuffs next to Jarrod in a few minutes, she might as well let it all out. "You saw what was going on here. He was forcing his own daughter to marry against her will when you guys raided the compound. He didn't care about her or any of his people. He only wanted power and control."

The agent rubbed his hand against his jaw. "So you hid her away to keep her safe?"

"Absolutely." And she'd do it again.

"That's what I'd figured you say," he said, his whole body relaxing from his on-duty stance. "I talked to the prosecutor a few minutes ago. We arrested the judge who issued your warrant while he was guarding the illegal armory. That definitely brings into question anything he may have done in a legal capacity to help the Crest Society and Fane. The prosecutor is quashing the warrant against you as we speak, so you don't have to worry about that anymore. And since this girl's daddy is headed off to prison for a very long time, I don't think he'll be in a place to contest your custody of her as willed by your sister."

A shaky laugh escaped and she leaned against Isaac, needing the support to stay standing on her suddenly weak legs. "I don't know what to say."

"Just don't ever come after me with a twirling baton and we'll call it even." The agent winked at her and nodded to Isaac before turning and walking back to the mass of ATF agents gathered near the armory.

Everything swam in her watery vision as Isaac wrapped his arms around her. A second set of arms encircled her. She reached out to curl her own arms around both Isaac and Essie. They'd done it. Everyone was safe. After a minute or an hour or an eternity, they broke apart. Each of them was grinning from ear to ear like idiots. Happy, happy idiots.

"So I guess that means I'm coming home with you, Aunt T," Essie said.

She nodded, almost too relieved to form words. "You bet."

"No more midnight makeovers with Uncle Albert then, huh?" The girl grinned and it had more than just a small spark of trouble to it.

"Don't worry, I'm sure you'll get to see plenty of him," Tamara said. "He's family."

"Can I call him? Let him know we're okay?"

Isaac handed over his phone. "Go for it."

While Essie was chatting with Albert using lots of hand gestures, she and Isaac hung back, watching the now-full transport van drive off toward the gate. The only thing that would have made it better was if Amelia had lived to see it. As the van pulled farther away, Tamara let go of Isaac's hand and took a couple of steps to watch it go down the main road until it was out of sight.

Once even the small cloud of dust kicked up by the van's tires was no longer visible, she turned back to Isaac. She expected to find him just as relieved as she was, but judging by his pinched expression he was feeling something completely different.

"So, you're free now." He made an attempt at keeping his tone light, but didn't quite manage it. "You've got all that cash in your duffle bag in the hotel. You can go wherever you want now."

She could. The possibilities of it all made her giddy, but not in the way he was thinking. "The only place I want to be is with you."

His shoulders relaxed as he closed the distance between them. "That's the best news I've heard all day."

"Bet I can top it." She wound her arms around his neck and raised herself up on her tip toes bringing her lips close enough to his that they almost touched. "I love you, Isaac Camacho."

"I love you too." And he kissed her like a man who would always lead her true...and she believed it.

CHAPTER TWENTY-FIVE

Elisa

Finally finished with the Feds' questions, Elisa walked away from the hubbub outside the Crest Society chapel. The compound was actually kind of nice, with all of the trees and the mountains surrounding the place. Might even be worth a vacation. Not that she ever took one of those. Vacations were not her thing. Life was boring if you weren't running from one firefight to another.

She didn't mean to walk over to Marko. It just happened. He was off in a quiet corner behind the chapel—exactly the kind of spot she was looking for after answering the same five questions from the Feds over and over for the past hour.

He had his back to her with his phone pressed up against his ear, giving her the perfect view of his wide shoulders, softball-sized biceps and his nice, round ass. Why did such a know-it-all have to come in that sweet, sweet package?

"Gillie, this isn't the best time. Let me call you ba—" Marko turned around, the look on his face anything but nice. He looked downright scary. "What do you mean, trouble?"

Elisa perked up. She couldn't help it. The sort of trouble that gave Marko that kind of face was her favorite.

"What do you mean you're there with Flynn?" Marko yanked on his beard as his eyes narrowed into mean little slits. "He's the last asshole you should be with." He paused to listen, then huffed out a frustrated breath. "Yeah, I know he's my friend. That doesn't mean I want my little sister hanging out with him."

Oh yes. Now this was some juicy gossip. Wait until she told the rest of the girls. Vivi was going to have a field day busting his balls about being an overprotective older brother. Not that she'd be alone in doing that. Nope. Elisa planned on taking more than a few shots herself.

"I have the B-Squad jet," Marko said into the phone. "I'll be there as soon as I can. Try not to blow the place up."

He hung up and shoved the phone into the left pocket of his jeans—no doubt because he dressed right. So she'd looked. What was he gonna do, sue her for checking him out? By the time her gaze made it back up to Marko's face, he was grinding his teeth down to nubs.

She just smiled. "Explosives, like literally?"

"With my sister?" He pinched the bridge of his nose and shook his head. "Anything is possible. I gotta go."

She fell into step beside him. "Not without me."

He picked up his pace, which was a real asshole thing to do because his legs were about twice the length of hers.

She didn't let it get to her, she just did a little walk-jog step to keep up. "Last time I checked, I was the only one of the two of us who had a pilot's license."

Marko's step faltered, but he kept moving forward. "I can catch a ride with the Feds."

"Not likely. All those thorny rules and regulations. You know you wouldn't be allowed to take your favorite toys if you did that. You know, the ones you definitely don't want the ATF to know about?"

He stopped so fast that she almost slammed into him. Reaching out, she wrapped her fingers around as much of his bicep as she could just to keep her balance. He glared down at her. If he was trying to intimidate her, he was using the wrong tack. She'd grown up at the feet of the master of surliness.

Cocking her head to the side, she gave him the extra bright smile she'd used when conning drunk bankers. "If you want to be airborne, looks like you're stuck with me."

"I don't have time for this," he grumbled.

"Then we'd better get moving." She hooked her arm through his and tried to tug him forward. He, of course, didn't budge. "I can't wait to meet your sister. I bet she knows all the dirt."

And Elisa couldn't wait to find out every little detail.

Marko mumbled something that sounded a lot like "God help me", but he started walking again. Oh, he could pray all he wanted to, but she was finally going to get something to lord over his head for the next time he went all sexy armchair psychiatrist on her.

CHAPTER TWENTY-SIX

Isaac
Two Months Later

There was no a pool outside the back door. There was no million-dollar art on the walls. There wasn't a single piece of wicker furniture anywhere in sight. And Isaac couldn't be happier.

"Please God, tell me that's the last one."

He looked over the top of the box labeled "clothes" that he was carrying from his truck to Tamara's house—scratch that—their house. She stood on the wide front porch of the 1920's-era Craftsman with a glass of wine in one hand and a beer in the other. Essie was visiting her uncle Albert in Hamilton for the four-day weekend, which made the timing perfect for the official move—not that anyone was shocked it was finally happening.

Vivi won the five-hundred dollar betting pool about when he and Tamara would finally move in together. Keir offered to help her spend it, but she'd told him she didn't play with pretty boys. Those two were neck and neck with Marko and Elisa in the new office pool about who would be next to follow Taz and Bianca—and now him and Tamara—into coupledom.

"This is it." He strolled up the sidewalk and set the box on the iron bistro table next to the front door so he could accept the beer.

Tamara cocked her head and stared at the box. "Why is there a picture of a baby drawn on the side?"

He almost choked on the beer in his mouth.

She did not...

He circled around the table.

Yes. Yes, she did.

He let out a sigh. Really, it was best Tamara learned about his family up front. "That's my mom's idea of being subtle."

"Wow," she said, not bothering to hold back her laugh.

"Just wait until we're married." Shit. He hadn't meant to say that. Not yet anyway.

Her eyes went wide, but she recovered half a second later. It took more than a mention of marriage to throw his girl.

She arched an eyebrow and took a sip of her wine. "What makes you think I'd say yes?"

He took a step closer to her, reaching out and tilting her chin up. It put her sweet mouth at just the right angle for what he wanted. "I know for a fact you get all hot and bothered for cocky Texans with big trucks."

"Is that what I like to be big?"

"You know it, darlin'." He dipped his head lower wanting—needing—to touch her.

"You never know. I might just surprise you." She pulled back before he could land the kiss and spun out of reach toward the door. "In fact, I've got one for you right now."

"Does it involve getting naked?" Please say yes.

She gave him that small smile of hers that said she knew exactly what he wanted to hear. "Mostly naked."

"What are you leaving on?" The answer was almost as important as what she was taking off.

"That's the surprise." She winked at him as she opened the screen door. "Meet me in the bedroom in five minutes."

"Sweeter words have never been spoken."

She laughed. "You are so full of it."

"And you love it."

Her smile flattened and her eyes lost that teasing glint. "I do."

She meant it. For the first time in both of their lives, they both did. There was no better moment then right now.

He reached into his pocket and took out the engagement ring that had been in his family for generations.

"Enough to say yes?" He lowered down to one knee. He'd been carrying the diamond ring around for the past two weeks, but the timing just never seemed right. Since he'd joined the B-Squad as an official member, he'd been working case after case. Tamara had been right, they'd needed him. Just like he'd needed her. This sure as hell wasn't where he'd expected to be a few months ago, but he was damn glad to be here. "The day we met I promised I'd only lead you true. In reality, it was you who showed me exactly where I needed to be…here with you. I love you Tamara Post. Will you marry me?"

The smile was back, bigger than ever. "Yes."

He slid the ring on her finger and gathered her up in his arms. When he kissed her this time it wasn't for today or tomorrow. It was for forever and everything that went with it. Kids. Family. The whole crazy mess.

When they finally broke apart, his first instinct was to pick her up caveman-style and take her into the house before the neighbors got one hell of a show. She had other ideas. She handed him his beer and took her wine glass, holding it up in a toast.

"To no more sad stories," she said, her voice shaking with emotion.

He sat down his beer and took her in his arms, knowing he'd never let her go. "Only happy endings."

Thank you so much for reading Bang! I hope you liked Tamara, Isaac, and the rest of the B-Squad team. If you have a second to leave a review, that would be awesome.

Next up in the B-Squad series is Blade. This will be Marko's little sister, Gillie's story and will come out in March as part of the Hot on Ice charity anthology featuring 19 sexy hockey stories. Don't worry, there will be plenty of B-Squad action in Blade. Then, get ready for Marko's and Elisa's story, Bold, in 2017. Both will be full of all the action, hotness and sass you expect from a B-Squad book.

Subscribe to my newsletter and you'll be the first to know when these new B-Squad books are available. Plus you'll get the latest book news, be able to enter monthly giveaways and more! Please stay in touch (avery@averyflynn.com), I love hearing from readers. Don't forget to check out my other books for more sexy, sassy romance!

xoxo,
Avery

ABOUT THE AUTHOR

Award-winning romance author Avery Flynn has three slightly-wild children, loves a hockey-addicted husband and is desperately hoping someone invents the coffee IV drip.

She was a reader before she was a writer and hopes to always be both. She loves to write about smartass alpha heroes who are as good with a quip as they are with their *ahem* other God-given talents. Her heroines are feisty, fierce and fantastic. Brainy and brave, these ladies know how to stand on their own two feet and knock the bad guys off theirs.

Find out more about Avery on her website, follow her on Twitter and Pinterest, like her on her Facebook page or friend her on her Facebook profile. She's also on Goodreads and BookLikes.
Join her street team, The Flynnbots, and receive special sneak peeks, prizes and early access to her latest releases!

Also, if you figure out how to send Oreos through the Internet, she'll be your best friend for life.

Contact her at avery@averyflynn.com. She'd love to hear from you!

ALSO BY AVERY FLYNN

The B-Squad Series
Bulletproof
Brazen (B-Squad 1)
Bang (B-Squad 2)
Blade (B-Squad 2.5) - Coming March 2017

The Killer Style Series
High-Heeled Wonder (Killer Style 1)
This Year's Black (Killer Style 2)
Make Me Up (Killer Style 3)
Designed For Murder (Killer Style 4)

The Laytons Series
Dangerous Kiss (Laytons 1)
Dangerous Flirt (Laytons 2)
Dangerous Tease (Laytons 3)

The Retreat Series
Dodging Temptation (The Retreat Book 1)

The Sweet Salvation Brewery Series
Enemies on Tap (Sweet Salvation Brewery 1)
Hollywood on Tap (Sweet Salvation Brewery 2)
Trouble on Tap (Sweet Salvation Brewery 3)

Novellas
Hot Dare (Dare to Love)
Daring Ink (Dare to Love)
Betting the Billionaire
Jax and the Beanstalk Zombies (Fairy True 1)
Big Bad Red (Fairy True 2)

Made in the USA
Lexington, KY
28 June 2017

ALSO BY AVERY FLYNN

The B-Squad Series
Bulletproof
Brazen (B-Squad 1)
Bang (B-Squad 2)
Blade (B-Squad 2.5) - Coming March 2017

The Killer Style Series
High-Heeled Wonder (Killer Style 1)
This Year's Black (Killer Style 2)
Make Me Up (Killer Style 3)
Designed For Murder (Killer Style 4)

The Laytons Series
Dangerous Kiss (Laytons 1)
Dangerous Flirt (Laytons 2)
Dangerous Tease (Laytons 3)

The Retreat Series
Dodging Temptation (The Retreat Book 1)

The Sweet Salvation Brewery Series
Enemies on Tap (Sweet Salvation Brewery 1)
Hollywood on Tap (Sweet Salvation Brewery 2)
Trouble on Tap (Sweet Salvation Brewery 3)

Novellas
Hot Dare (Dare to Love)
Daring Ink (Dare to Love)
Betting the Billionaire
Jax and the Beanstalk Zombies (Fairy True 1)
Big Bad Red (Fairy True 2)

Made in the USA
Lexington, KY
28 June 2017